Ransomed by Kashatok

A Steamy Sci Fi Alien Romance

Galactic Pirate Brides
Book Two

Tamsin Ley

Twin Leaf Press

To my amazing beta readers, Shanda, Shawna, Diane, and Vinita. Thank you for your patience, input, and butt-kicking on a book that took forever to write.

Chapter One

Facing the cantina's dirty restroom mirror, Joy gripped a hunk of her curly brown hair in one hand and scissors in the other. Behind her, a wall-length screen flickered with an ad for inter-alien contraceptive products, haloing her with eerie green light.

Just do it, she thought. *Hair grows back, no big deal.* Except that her mother, a Syndicorp Communications CEO, already liked to goad her about her fashion sense, saying it was a good thing Joy was smart, because she'd never get by on her looks. Yet even being smart wasn't good enough, not unless Joy used it to climb the corporate ladder.

When Joy signed on as a reporter with RealTime News, her mother'd almost disowned her. How was she going to react when she found out Joy was doing an undercover exposé? *At least I'm not disguising myself as a prosti-tute.* Not that her producer at RealTime hadn't hinted at how sensational *that* would be. But Joy had tools other than her tits to secure this story. Being tall for a woman, she'd decided to go the complete opposite direction with her disguise. Her canvas cargo pants and mechanic shirt were boxy and genderless, and she'd even gone so far as to wrap her breasts to mask her curves.

She just needed the finishing touch.

Taking a deep breath, she squeezed the scissors. Her long tresses fell away with an oddly satisfying sensation. A lopsided reflection stared back at her with startled brown eyes. "No going back now," she muttered.

Her square jaw wasn't quite manly, but she was plain enough that with the right attitude, she could pass for a boy. And she'd already proven she had attitude doing a year of volunteer work for Syndicorp's planetary emergency services division in their fleet mechanic shop. Joy'd loved the hands-on problem-solving and the smell of hydraulic fluid and hot metal until Mother learned she wasn't handing out cookies and pulled her.

Satisfied with her hair, Joy pulled mascara out of her purse and dabbed it beneath her nails, rubbing it into her skin for good measure. No one trusted a mechanic with clean hands. When she was satisfied, she once again looked into the mirror, winking her left eye to engage her cybernetic camera. A recording of her reflection would make a decent, gritty opening scene for the exposé. One benefit of having a Communications CEO for a mother was that Joy had access to technology other newbie reporters would die for.

"I'm at the edge of unclassified space, looking for information about pirate activity. These ruthless men and women have been plaguing the shipping lanes since Syndicorp sent its first colonization envoys outside the Aleigh system." Joy spoke in a husky, conspiratorial tone, glancing over her shoulder at the restroom door. The chances of someone entering were slim to none with the hotel door grav-loc she'd placed against the door stop, but her pulse beat loudly in her ears even so. "Stay tuned as I go undercover into the swashbuckling world of black market trading and deep-space piracy—bleh."

Sighing, she stopped the camera. She sounded like a game show host. Everything about this broadcast had to be perfect. Serious. Anchor-worthy.

She tried again. "My informant just sent word there's a notorious pirate in this very bar. I'm going to try to join his crew. For the next few weeks, I'll be broadcasting the RealTime stories of these men."

The door rattled. Joy quickly cached the recordings on her polycom to edit later and removed the grav-loc, brushing past the annoyed saluqan woman outside. "Watch it. Door sticks," Joy mumbled and dove into the crowded cantina. She had a pirate captain to find.

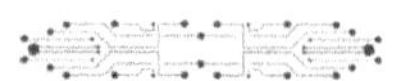

Captain Kashatok pried Jhikik's tail from around the bottle of Kantarellian rum and poured himself another tall serving. On board ship, he often drank straight from the bottle. For the purpose of interviewing new crew members, he was attempting to look civilized. He had enough rough edges on his crew, and attracting yet another discipline problem was not in his plan today.

The little netorpok chittered at him in reprimand and climbed up his arm to sit on his shoulder, his lavender fur tickling Kashatok's ear. Jhikik had come into his possession as a pup, and, much like an actual child, liked to nag him about his vice. "Keep it down."

Too late. A woman who'd been perched on a stool at the bar was heading in his direction, her sizable cleavage jiggling above the low neckline of her tight blouse with every step. Happened every time. First, she'd fawn over the netorpok, then turn her attention to the broad-shouldered owner. Women loved a man with a pet. And Jhikik loved the attention.

"There's a reason I never leave the ship," Kashatok muttered, glowering at the woman. Female company was never on his agenda and never would be.

Thankfully, the oncoming woman took the hint and veered toward the restrooms. As the cantina's band started up a new set, Kashatok rose from his chair and scanned the dark interior of the cantina for his first mate's shaggy head. Aleknagik was supposed to be escorting prospective shuttle mechanics to the table for interviews. Across the dimly lit floor, cantina patrons parted like an outgoing tide around the tall, copper-skinned denaidan. *About time he found someone.* Settling back into his chair, Kashatok downed the rest of the rum in his glass. Aleknagik pulled up to the table and stopped.

Kashatok scanned the conspicuously empty space around to the big man. "Well?"

Aleknagik shook his head. "Word's gotten around about what happened to our last mechanic."

The muscle in Kashatok's jaw tightened. "And?"

"No one's exactly excited to be the next one tossed out the airlock."

"I have one hard rule. No women aboard my ship." Not only that, but what the mechanic had been doing to that poor female deserved retribution.

Sliding out a chair, Aleknagik sat heavily, the reek of cirripi weed wafting off him. He leaned forward, both elbows on the table. "Listen, I understand why you made that rule. But with those nanites Captain Qaiyaan's been talking about, we might be able to change that. Plus, your non-denaidan crew members might appreciate some leeway."

Kashatok gritted his teeth. The *Kinship*'s core crew of denaidans could not enjoy the pleasures of women, and Kashatok's rule had never made much of a difference to them. Until the nanites. Once again, Syndicorp had planted a seed of hope within the denaidans. No, not a seed. A spore. A *virus*. A Syndicorp engineered virus. And it was fucking with his ship. "My ship—my rules. If someone's not okay with that, they can get the fuck off."

His first mate frowned but kept silent, his eyes full of questions and distrust.

Grabbing the rum, Kashatok took a long pull of the burning liquid. There'd never be a woman for him, anyway, nanites or not. He couldn't be trusted, not after Aiyana… He took another swallow. His past was none of Aleknagik's business.

An olive-skinned human appeared just past Aleknagik's shoulder, wide brown eyes darting between the back of the first mate's head and Kashatok. The moment their eyes met, Kashatok felt a jolt, a desire to protect that was at odds with the hard-assed captain he tried to be. The kid reminded him of his own first insecure days off-planet, seeking jobs in seedy cantinas just like this one. The visitor moved up beside the first mate, both hands shoved deep in the front pockets of his baggy cargo pants. "You're looking for a shuttle mechanic?"

Aleknagik twisted in his seat, eyes nearly level with their visitor's. "You know one?"

The young man stretched a hand forward. "Name's Joey."

"You?" Aleknagik laughed.

Jhikik leaped from Kashatok's shoulder onto the table-top. Kashatok snatched hold of the tip of the creature's tail, drawing him up short. Not everyone appreciated the creature's curiosity.

Turning to Kashatok, Aleknagik jerked a thumb toward Joey, eyes dancing with mirth. "What do you say, Captain? Think this *qumli* could hold his own among our crew?"

The kid was barely old enough to leave his mother's teat, let alone stand up to a rowdy crew. Kashatok sent out a tightly controlled ionic pulse. Alcohol dulled his sensitivity, but he could still assess the kid's heartbeat, breathing, and skin temperature. Joey was nervous, for sure. But his hands were dirty, and the look in his eye was hungry. Would it hurt to let him have his say? Kashatok pushed the rum bottle forward without accepting the handshake. "Have a seat."

Dropping his hand, Joey pulled out a chair and sat. He didn't touch the rum. They locked gazes, and Kashatok had to hand it to him—the kid didn't look away. "You don't seem old enough to be a mechanic."

Joey shrugged one shoulder. "Only been at it a year, but I'm a fast learner."

Kashatok retrieved the bottle and tilted back for a long swallow. May as well let the kid see the real him. "You familiar with the CrossX Spacer Elite?"

"Sure." Joey tilted his head and squinted his eyes in thought. "I helped with a thruster rebuild. And adjusted the flux coil on one of the newer models."

"Huh," said Aleknagik, nodding. "Where're you from?"

Joey scowled. "Why's that matter?"

Aleknagik dropped his bearded chin to glower back. Jhikik crept forward, eyes on the stranger.

"What?" Joey crossed his arms. "Pirates don't have pasts. Or they shouldn't."

Kashatok repressed a smile. This kid might just be capable of holding his own after all. He stroked his fingertips along Jhikik's long tail until the little creature spun and batted at his hand. "You heard about our last mechanic?"

The young man's left eye twitched. "Tell me."

"Space-locked." Kashatok paused a moment. Joey's heart beat so rapidly, Kashatok barely had to engage his ionic senses to feel it.

"By you?"

Kashatok nodded slowly, keeping eye contact. "There's only one unbreakable rule on the *Kinship*. You can't bring women on board. Think you can handle that?"

Joey took a long breath and let it out slowly. "That's all? Sounds easy. What's my cut?"

"Ha!" Aleknagik clapped the young man on the shoulder, rocking him forward. "I like him!"

Joey kept his gaze on the captain.

For some reason, Kashatok hadn't expected the mercenary question, probably because the kid had seemed more interested in the adventure than the money. "Probation gets you one share. Things work out after the first score or two, we'll talk more."

Nodding, Joey once again thrust out his hand. "Deal."

This time, Kashatok took it. The palm was softer than he'd expected, but maybe that was just a human thing. "We're parked in slip A21P. I'll be pulling out as soon as we're restocked, so I suggest you get your ass aboard sooner rather than later."

"Aye aye, captain."

Alek laughed again. "We don't say that, human."

Joey licked his lips, and Kashatok found the move oddly disturbing. "Sorry," said the kid. "I do call you captain though, right?"

"I don't care what you call me, as long as you do your job." Kashatok rose, grabbing the rum bottle and holding out an arm for Jhikik. The netorpok gave Joey a longing look, then skittered up to rest on Kashatok's shoulder.

As Kashatok turned to leave, Joey called out, "I'll keep your shuttle in top shape."

Kashatok kept moving. Behind him, he heard Alek giving advice. "Young man like you's got urges. Long as you take care of them off-ship, you'll be fine. Oh, and stay away from the captain's rum."

Stopping at the crowded bar, Kashatok ordered one last bottle to go.

CHAPTER TWO

Joy dodged a six-legged yanipa-nimayu bulling its way through the crowd and halted to allow an armed rakwiji to cross to a nearby cantina. Ahead, above the throng, a beat-up sign pointed toward slip A21P. A posungi reeking of cirripi weed brushed against her, facial tentacles waving, and she gripped her satchel tighter, wary of pickpockets. Her time volunteering with Syndicorp's emergency services division had exposed her to some rough men, but nothing like the throng pressing around her now. Hoping things improved once she was on board the ship, she kept her head up and strode forward with purpose. Sometimes just appearing to look like you knew what you were doing was enough to deter trouble.

She reached the docking corridor connecting the station to the ship, expecting a guard or someone to greet her.

The entrance was wide open and vacant. Interesting. Kashatok was obviously very confident with his reputation. She'd done a few minutes of preliminary research before heading over and learned that he and his crew specialized in hijacking entire ships, scrapping them, and selling out the parts. As the new shuttle mechanic, she'd likely soon be doing the same. She'd hoped to get more background on the big, copper-skinned alien who was to be her captain—she'd never encountered a man like him before—but there were surprisingly few records on him.

Well, that would change with this exposé. Squeezing her left eye, she took a few still shots of the open entry. She could add some narrative later.

She stepped into the docking corridor, her heart hammering. The captain's rule about no women on board had almost made her change her mind. But after asking around in the cantina, she'd learned more about the crewman she was replacing. He'd brought a woman on board, and Kashatok'd set the woman free, ejecting only his offending crew member into space. The other woman probably hadn't known the rule, but Joy had been warned. What would happen if she was discovered? Would he space-lock her? Her stomach churned. Maybe she should turn around. It wasn't too late. No one had seen her.

A tug on her pant leg drew her attention from the dimly lit cargo bay ahead. Something scurried up the folds of her cargo pants, little claws digging through the fabric to prick her skin. She let out a squeak, stiffening as a set of dark eyes stopped within inches of hers, staring up from its hold on her chest.

The captain's pet.

She regained her balance and stared back, hardly daring to breathe. Just because it was adorable didn't mean it was friendly. The face had a row of small horns set between its eyes and its feathery-looking ears fluttered. Was it just allowed to run free? At least she didn't see any exposed teeth.

Nose wriggling, it sniffed her, flicking its long, furry tail back and forth. The flattened end curved up over its shoulder toward her, revealing octopus-like suction cups on the underside. She laughed nervously as the fuzzy tip stroked her jawline. She'd never been allowed to have a pet, but her friends had owned species of varying friendliness. Keeping her fingers curled inward in case the thing decided to bite, she ran her knuckles along its lavender-furred shoulder. "Hello, little fellow. What's your name?"

The creature made a little "jweek jweek" sound and closed its eyes.

She opened her hand and stroked the feather-soft fur. "Is your master aboard?"

In answer, it clambered the rest of the way up her chest and settled on her shoulder, long tail wrapping gently around her throat. It closed its eyes and settled down as if to sleep.

"Okay, then." Strangely fortified by the greeting, she continued into the cargo bay. A beat-up CrossX Spacer Elite sat to one side of a dimly lit, industrial-gray area. She breathed deeply, relieved she'd taken a few minutes to download Syndicorp's specs for the shuttle. Her accessibility to the galactic web after she was on board was uncertain, and she needed to look like she knew what she was doing. Against the far wall, two open airlocks provided her no guidance.

"There you are." A deep voice made her spin, and she collided with a broad chest smelling of sweet rum and ginger. Her gaze roamed upward from the silver-banded dark beard bisecting the captain's chest to his firm but sensuous mouth. She wasn't used to feeling so short. His hair, pulled into a top-knot, exposed silver earrings, and one strand had come loose to hang between his intense, obsidian eyes. Had he been waiting for her? An unfamiliar yet exciting thrill fluttered in the pit of her stomach.

"Come here, Jhikik." He plucked the little creature from her shoulder, taking no more notice of her than if she'd been a tree.

He was looking for his pet, not waiting for her. The strange feeling in her stomach subsided. She adjusted her satchel. "What kind of animal is that?"

He settled the creature on his own shoulder where it chittered loudly. "Netorpok."

"I've never heard of it."

"Endangered species." He adjusted its tail around his neck as if it was choking him. "Banned on most worlds."

"Oh." Joy tried to be nonchalant, but there could be another story here. Some exotic pets were banned because their intelligence made them more like slaves than pets. "Is he sentient?"

Kashatok shook his head and rubbed two knuckles along the creature's forehead on either side of its horns. "Though sometimes I wonder."

His gaze shifted to her for the first time since she'd bumped into him. Her breath caught. She'd never been particularly attracted to bad boys, but this pirate's attention made her quiver low in her belly. "Um, where should I put my stuff?"

A muscle in the side of the captain's jaw twitched and his copper skin darkened with a slightly blue-green tinge. He took a long drink from the bottle in his other hand. "Bunk room's down that corridor behind you."

Bunk room? Joy's throat grew tight. Passing for a guy would become exponentially more difficult if she had to share quarters with a bunch of other men. What if they took communal showers or something? She hadn't thought this through very well. "I don't get my own quarters?"

"You could." The first mate's voice startled her from behind. She jumped, nearly stepping on Kashatok's toes. "A private room'll cost you your share, though." Aleknagik leaned against the corridor exit, arms crossed over his chest.

Relief flooded her. Little did they know she didn't need the money. In fact, she'd pay extra for a private room if it wouldn't blow her cover. But she was supposed to be a greedy pirate here, so she pretended to pause and consider. "My entire share?"

"Actually, two shares." Kashatok's voice at her back held a note of warning.

She swallowed, feeling trapped between the two men. "But I only get one share."

"Exactly." Kashatok glowered over the top of her head at his first mate. "Aleknagik shouldn't get your hopes up."

Aleknagik pushed himself off the wall and took a step closer. He was just as big and copper-skinned as the captain, although instead of keeping his hair pulled up into a queue, he'd braided it into several rows along his scalp, leaving the back portion as wildly unkempt as the vast beard covering his chest. "Syndicorp's breathing down our necks, captain. We don't have time to find a new mechanic."

Joy clutched her satchel tightly against her chest. They needed a mechanic, and that gave her leverage; a real pirate would probably ask for more at this moment. Calming her breathing so she could speak, she squeaked out, "I want three shares."

Kashatok lifted an eyebrow, and she swore she saw a smile lurking at the corner of his mouth. "Don't push your luck, kid." He took another long drink, then once again pierced her with his dark eyes. "One share, and you can sleep in a storeroom by yourself. Fair enough?"

Wondering what he'd look like if he really smiled, Joy nodded. She'd pushed enough to appear genuine, and she'd gotten what she really needed to make it to the next port without blowing her cover.

Kashatok spun without another word and strode down the nearest corridor, surprisingly steady for someone who'd just consumed almost half a bottle of rum.

"This way," Aleknagik said, walking toward the opposite corridor.

Joy jogged after him, glancing over her shoulder toward the corridor the captain had taken. Before she left this ship, she was going to get the captain to smile for the camera. He was going to make a fabulous centerpiece for her exposé.

Kashatok leaned back in his desk chair and stared out the view screen at the scatter of ships coming and going from the berths as the *Kinship* pulled away from the station. The sporadic burbling from the hydroponic garden in one corner of his sitting room did little to calm him. He pulled another bottle of Kantarellian rum from his desk drawer. He hated the exposure of the docks and itched to hit the burn drives. The empty coldness of space was preferable. If he didn't need to offload goods and pick up intel or let his men blow off steam, he'd be happy to never leave the confines of his ship.

He took a long drink to calm his anxiety, relishing the heat hitting his stomach. Another thing that made him edgy was that new shuttle mechanic. Something about the kid had Kashatok's mind going places it shouldn't— like the idea of him sharing a bunk with the other members of the crew. In lieu of female company, his two human crewmen were not above scratching each other's itches. As far as he knew, it was consensual, but who knew what might happen with the introduction of someone as young and fresh as Joey? A core part of him had been relieved to offer separate sleeping arrangements, even if some of the crew might grumble about preferential treatment.

Needing to stop dwelling on the new crew member, he dug in his pocket and retrieved the data chip his cartel contact had handed him on his way out of the cantina. While most denaidans were ex-troopers, he'd been with the cartel since long before Syndicorp had terminated Denaida-daru. The cartel hadn't cared that his people considered him a monster. That he'd left his world in shame. Only now, with his race all but extinct, had his denaidan brothers accepted him back into the fold.

Or perhaps they didn't remember.

Whatever the reason, it hardly mattered to Kashatok. For a fee, he shared his cartel information with the rest of the fleet, keeping the top-level intel for himself. The chip he held now was fresh off Syndicorp's servers, not even on the darkweb yet, and should hold information about some decent scores. Plugging the data chip into his desk monitor, he perused ship stats, gauged distances and travel times, and calculated the value of the posted manifests.

He crossed off passenger ships and colonist charters, preferring to target ships transporting commodities or bulk electronics, which were easier to cash out. One ship on the list looked promising, a K-class freighter routed between the mining strips within the Brandton asteroid belt. Problem was, it was at least three burn cycles away. He sighed. Denaidans could do the jump in a single burn, but his posungi gunner was extra sensitive to long burns and his two—now three—humans wouldn't respond much better. Plus, he wanted to break the new mechanic in slowly.

Sending the coordinates to the bridge, he glanced out the view screen at the thinning traffic. The ship would take another hour to clear the station's burn buffer. "Think our new crew member's settled in, Jhikik?"

Kashatok didn't usually fraternize with his crew, but events of late seemed to be pushing him to pay more attention. First, he'd caught his previous mechanic performing sadistic acts of pleasure with a woman in the ship's weapon locker—while they were in port, no less. Kashatok suspected some crew members had even known, but he couldn't prove it. The way some of them talked about females made him queasy. But as long as things didn't happen aboard his ship, it wasn't his responsibility; everything and everyone aboard this vessel was.

His mind returned to the crew's most recent addition. *Ellam Cua*, his fucking men better all be getting along.

Grabbing the rum in one hand, he held out the other. A little more attentiveness by the *Kinship's* captain was long overdue. "Come on, Jhik."

The netorpok scurried up his arm and settled on his shoulder.

Exiting his stuffy cabin, Kashatok headed toward the galley. The smell of broiled kemeg wafted down the hall, and Chignik's laughter echoed from the galley's open door. *Good.* He'd been correct assuming that's where they usually gathered. He hoped laughter meant everyone was getting along.

As he passed the door to engineering, Joey stepped out, almost colliding with him. "Oh!" The kid drew up short, blinking at him before attempting a smile. "Hi, Captain."

Jhikik chirped and scurried half-way down Kashatok's arm toward the new crewman, long tail twitching.

Hindered by the bottle in one hand, Kashatok snatched at the creature. His crew tolerated the netorpok, but the men could be less-than-gentle on the rare occasions Jhikik chose to interact with them—usually because he was running away with one of their socks.

Joey opened both hands to catch him, but Jhikik scurried over the kid's head, his tail forcing Joey to scrunch his eyes closed. "Always wanted a pet."

"He's more of a companion than a pet." Kashatok surprised himself with his own jovial candor. He was accustomed to protecting Jhikik from a disgruntled crewman and occasionally dodging a cantina female. Joey was neither, yet the netorpok seemed to like him. *Score one for the kid.* Kashatok's mouth twitched into a wry smile. "And he's usually far more loyal."

Joey laughed and pulled Jhikik's tail away from his mouth. "He's just curious."

Aren't we all? thought Kashatok. But one thing he'd learned during his years with the cartel was not to ask questions. Questions led to questions, and Kashatok had no desire to provide answers about himself. "Crew usually gathers in the galley between burns. You coming?"

Joey nodded emphatically. "Gassy went on ahead. Said he needed to soften the crew up before I got there for a game of cards." He chewed his bottom lip. "But I've got nothing to wager."

Distracted by the kid's bottom lip, Kashatok turned toward the galley. "Never admit that. A pirate must always bet more than he has."

"Got it." Joey hustled to keep up beside him. "I'm gonna use that line someday. So, what should I bet?"

Kashatok immediately thought of several bawdy suggestions and bit his tongue. Bad enough the kid would get it from the crew. He didn't need to be ribbed by his captain as well. "You seem fairly proficient with a spanner. How about I float you a loan, and you can do some maintenance on my hydroponic system? Know anything about those?"

The kid shrugged, loosening Jhikik's tail from its stranglehold around his neck. "I know pumps and thermostats. That's all hydroponics is."

"There you go then. I'll front you a few credits."

Joey grinned at him, and Kashatok suddenly needed a drink. Luckily, he still held the bottle in one hand. He took a couple of swallows and avoided looking at the kid until they reached the galley.

Inside, Gassy, the ship's grizzled denaidan engineer, sat at one end of the U-shaped table slapping down cards with Ekwok and Chignik. Chignik threw his cards down and leaned back in his chair, crossing his copper-skinned arms over his chest. "*Anaq*, you beat me every time, Gassy."

The engineer swept his gnarled copper hands out to gather the cards, tapping them into a pile. "Benefits of age and experience, my friend. Your deal, Ekwok."

Shaking his buff-colored mane of hair, Ekwok took the cards and glanced toward the door. When he spotted Kashatok, he half rose from his seat. "Captain? Something wrong?"

From the cushioned seats in the entertainment alcove, Aleknagik twisted to look over his shoulder. Manopup's orange-tentacled face rose above the back of another chair. "Captain?"

Skin heating, Kashatok moved forward and set his bottle at an open spot among the gamers. "Just thought I'd make sure the new crewman's fitting in. Deal me in."

The crew blinked at him for an uncomfortable heartbeat before settling warily back in their seats. He'd come to keep things settled. Hopefully his presence wouldn't rile them up instead.

Gassy looked past Kashatok toward Joey and tapped the tabletop next to him. "Saved you a seat, kid. Know how to play Ongaru Flip?"

Joey raised an eyebrow and sidled over. "Used to beat my supervisor all the time back on Tenben."

As the kid took a seat, a small part of Kashatok surged with jealousy at the easy camaraderie. *You shouldn't be surprised. These men work together.* He also shouldn't be a stranger on his own ship.

Ekwok dealt the cards, and Kashatok handed a few credits to Joey to start off. That got him some raised eyebrows, but no one said anything. After several rounds, Joey'd won eighty-two credits and Chignik's promise to take over Joey's next shift cleaning the bathrooms. Gassy tossed in his hand and rose. "This old man's out. Going to catch a few winks before we burn."

Jhikik bounded across the table as if chasing him away, sending cards fluttering to the floor in his wake.

"Little *tunrak*," Chignik swore. "Go find some socks to chew."

The netorpok chittered and disappeared into the hallway ahead of Gassy.

Ekwok shoved his cards to the center of the table. "Gotta go, too. It's my shift on the bridge. Good playing with you, Captain."

Kashatok scooped a few cards from the floor. He had to admit, this was more fun than pacing his cabin and watching Jhikik try to pull naujiar leaves through the hydroponic cage. "Chignik, Joey, you still in?"

Chignik shook his head. "One turn cleaning bathrooms is enough for me."

Joey remained seated. "I'll do one more round."

Suddenly nervous, Kashatok glanced at the entertainment alcove. "Aleknagik, Manopup, either of you in?"

No answer but a snore.

With only two players, the game became more difficult, and in the first two hands, Joey lost everything except Chignik's writ to clean the bathrooms.

Kashatok settled back. "Looks like you're out of currency. And captains are exempt from bathroom cleaning."

Joey chewed his bottom lip, a habit Kashatok was still trying hard not to notice. "We never actually talked about a price to fix your hydroponic system. What's it worth to you?"

Kashatok plopped his rum on the table, realizing he hadn't finished the bottle. "You like rum?"

"Ordinary rum?" Joey rolled his eyes. "For my extraordinary skill and effort?"

That made Kashatok laugh. "All right. How about I cover the first payment for your private bunk?"

"Now you're talking." Joey snatched up another card.

Smirking, Kashatok countered Joey's next flip.

Joey hit back with a double reverse and closed out his hand for a winning blow. "Ha! That means at the end of this job, I get two full shares!"

"Two?" Kashatok tossed the remainder of his hand on the table and crossed his arms. The kid was nothing if not tenacious. "I'm pretty sure we agreed to one."

Joey lifted his chin, crossing his own scrawny arms. "A private bunk is worth two, you said."

Kashatok held back a smile. Two shares certainly wouldn't break him, but he couldn't appear to give in too easily. "Tell you what, you fix my hydroponics, and I'll give you three shares at the end of this job. How's that sound?"

"Deal." Joey thrust out one hand.

Taking the kid's small palm in his, Kashatok grinned. Assuming Joey really could fix the hydroponic system, Kashatok'd gotten the better end of the deal. He wondered what else he might be able to get Joey to fix.

Chapter Three

"Up and at 'em, kid."

Joy opened her eyes at the first mate's gruff voice, nausea rising in her throat. Two burn cycles in rapid succession were more than she was used to, and Gassy told her there would only be a short break between this one and the next. She pulled one arm free of the chair's compression cavity and rubbed her eyes. These seats weren't exactly the first class modules she was accustomed to. Her mother's private transport seldom traveled long distances, and the charters Joy'd used for longer journeys provided two or even three days between each burn to allow passengers time to recuperate.

Blinking to engage her camera, she glanced around at the rest of the crew. Of the ten other crewmen, seven of them were the same species as the captain—denaidan. She wondered why she'd never encountered their kind before. There had to be a story here. As soon as she had a private moment to access a comm, she planned to pull up some intel on denaidans. She pushed the chair's frequency modulators off her temples, recalling Kashatok leaping three meters into the air to a ledge no wider than her hand. Her female demographic would go gaga over that bit of footage.

Beside her, the single posungi crewman stumbled out of his chair, facial tentacles flushed more vibrantly orange than she remembered. The wiry human on his other side shoved a flexible container toward him. "Keep it off the floor this time, Manopup."

The posungi snatched the container and shoved his face into it just in time to wretch violently. Several crew members laughed, but Joy's stomach roiled as the putrid stench of vomit wafted her way.

"New-boy's looking a little peaked, too, Cooper. You got a bucket for him?" the second human commented, looking down his crooked nose at her. He was almost as tall as the copper-skinned crewmen, but his bald, tattooed head was a distinct contrast to the shaggy-haired aliens.

"I'm fine." She loosed the chair's restraints and pushed herself upright. She had to pee, but could hear the voices of other crewmen in the lavatory. Although she slept in the storeroom all by herself, she still had to share the other common rooms, and had needed to be very careful with her personal grooming over the last couple of days.

"Come on, kid," Gassy called from the doorway. "We need all systems optimized before the next burn."

Feeling a headache beginning, she turned off her camera and wobbled toward the door, leaving the gagging posungi and the two humans behind her.

In engineering, the air felt like a sauna. Gassy sent her into the twisted piping and thick conduits he called "the jungle" to manually adjust the burn drive's coolant system. Squeezed in among the valves and pipes, the air was even hotter and the hum of pumps and fans drowned out all other sounds. Sweat poured between her breasts, soaking the under-wrap that kept her chest flat. God, she felt like she was suffocating. What she wouldn't give for a shower right now. But she doubted she'd get enough privacy for a shower anytime in the near future.

At least the job was interesting, reminding her of her days with emergency services. She adjusted some valves, then ducked out to a nearby console to verify that the gauges matched the ship's computer readings. Everything was within tolerances. She shot a glance over her shoulder. Gassy was busy at the main engineering station and Moore'd just exited pushing a cart of supplies. Now was her chance for a quick bit of research without anyone looking over her shoulder.

Turning back to the console's comm interface, she typed a query about denaidans. Several suggested spellings popped up, plus a few personal profiles on people with the name Aiden, but no intel. *Strange.* She tried a different spelling. Deneyeden. Even fewer options. Den —eye-don. Nothing.

"Ahem." A throat cleared just behind her shoulder.

She spun, cheeks heating as she stared up into Gassy's bearded face. *You haven't done anything wrong—at least, not that he knows about,* she reminded herself. "Uh, whatcha need?"

"You won't find anything about denaidans on the galactic web."

Her throat felt tight. "Why's that?"

"Syndicorp controls the news services."

Mention of the media had her stomach doing flip flops

and reminded her to start recording. "Why would Syndicorp want to keep your race a secret?"

The lines around his eyes hardened. "Because they destroyed our planet and everyone on it."

She sucked in a breath and half turned to the comm as if it might refute his story. "That can't be true. I'd've heard of something like that."

He snorted and turned toward the cargo bay. "You underestimate the corp'. And with most off-world denaidans being troopers, it made it easy to eliminate the few people who cared about the Termination. Those who escaped, well… There're only about a hundred of us left in the entire galaxy."

She followed him out of engineering, her mind swimming with so many questions, she wasn't sure what to ask first. Pausing to pan the camera over several crew members prepping weapons and gear for the upcoming hijacking, she asked, "You were a trooper?"

"Aye." He continued past the men toward the bay door.

Taking a long, slow perusal of Kashatok sitting on an empty cargo pod with a long pulse rifle across his knees, she was startled when Aleknagik thrust the butt ends of two pulse pistols in her direction. "What's your preference?"

Her stomach lurched into her throat, and she stared at the guns. Did a shuttle mechanic also take part in the fighting? Once again, she realized she hadn't fully thought this plan through. She didn't think she could shoot someone, even if her life depended on it. Yet refusing to take part would certainly raise questions. Extending one shaky hand toward the smaller weapon, she tried to keep her voice low and steady. "What're we shooting?"

From across the bay, Kashatok called out. "The kid's staying on board."

Thank goodness. She flicked her gaze toward the captain once again. His intent stare made her insides flutter. With one hand, he reached absently for the rum beside him, but Jhikik chose that moment to leap to the floor, long tail toppling the bottle. The crash of breaking glass filled the cargo bay.

Kashatok rose, his face cut into deep scowl lines. "I ought to use you for target practice."

Jhikik scurried up Joy's pant leg, settling on her shoulder. His soft tail wrapped loosely around her neck as he peered around her head at his master.

Aleknagik guffawed. "What do you know? The little monster likes the new boy. Just watch your socks, kid."

One of Kashatok's eyes twitched in irritation. "Jhikik, come here."

Joy nudged the creature, but instead of moving, it purred in her ear. Maybe she could at least take some of the heat off the poor little thing. "Uh, you want me to clean up for you, captain?"

That only made Kashatok scowl more. "I can do my own cleaning. Gassy needs you. Go."

Turning, she hurried to the docking platform where Gassy stood watching the events. He surveyed Jhikik, still perched on her shoulder. "I guess you can work with him hanging around. Odd, though." The old engineer met her eye. "He doesn't generally like other men."

Her breath caught. He'd said men, not people. Did he suspect she was female? Looking for a quick change of subject, she tried to resume their previous conversation, her gaze drifting back toward Kashatok. "Was the captain a trooper, too?"

Gassy turned to the console and began pulling up sensor data. "Nope. He left Denaida-daru to join the cartel. Still the only cartel member in the fleet."

"Huh. I thought all pirates were part of the cartel."

He shook his head. "Rest of the fleet traded with the cartel in the past, but there's been some bad blood between us and them lately." He handed her a calibration unit and pointed to the bay door. "Take this over there."

Joy complied, following his instructions with ease. Her mind was on her exposé, which was turning into a bigger story than she'd first imagined. Every time she asked one question, a dozen more popped up. And she was still baffled that she'd been unable to pull up anything on the denaidans, especially if some of them had been troopers. A small piece of her had begun to fear that at least some of what Gassy claimed about Syndicorp might be true.

If it was true, there had to be records somewhere. Her mother was the Communications CEO; perhaps she could provide some clues, assuming Joy could catch her with her guard down. *What will she think if I blow open a major Syndicorp cover-up?* Part of Joy was terrified at the thought. The other part was rubbing her hands in glee.

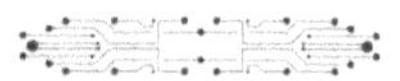

Kashatok woke at the sound of his alarm and reached for the rum, rinsing his mouth and swallowing before rising from his bed. He'd had to drink himself to sleep to clear the kid from his mind and hoped he didn't regret it during today's burn. Although he hadn't experienced a hangover in years, even he had limits. He rolled over, looking for Jhikik, who was usually in his face looking for breakfast. The little *tunrak* better not have started sleeping with the kid, too.

He found the netorpok chewing on a sock in the corner. "Really, Jhik? That's disgusting." Sighing, he retrieved the sock and tossed it into the recycle bin before opening the hydroponics cage and plucking a few naujiar leaves. "Here."

After checking the water and nutrient levels, he relocked the cage. His little friend couldn't be trusted with the plants any more than he could be trusted with the crew's socks, and the small garden was the creature's primary source of food. He was a little worried at the number of dying branches he'd been trimming. Soon as they'd finished this job, he'd get Joey in here to look at the thing.

Returning to the desk, he keyed his desk comm. "Aleknagik, we ready for final burn?"

"Uh, you're going to need to come down here and talk to Gassy about that."

"Why?" Kashatok drew out the word. Gassy'd been growing a little forgetful of late, but he'd been with the ship so long, Kashatok hesitated to retire him.

"There's something going on with the docking tube." In the background, raised voices sounded like they were arguing.

Grumbling, Kashatok jerked away from the desk and stalked toward the door. "Come on, Jhik."

The netorpok stuffed the last leaf in his mouth and leaped onto Kashatok's outstretched arm for the brisk walk to engineering. Gassy's voice echoed down the corridor from the cargo bay, his gruff tone underscored by a dull roar. "There's a differential in the hydraulic pressure you have to take into consideration when you make your adjustments."

Continuing past engineering, Kashatok paused at the threshold of the cargo bay. A flat piece that looked suspiciously like a piece of the docking ramp hung suspended from the ceiling. Gassy's broad-shouldered figure loomed beside someone short and thin. Each wore a blocky face shield, and Gassy directed the blue flame of a welding torch along a portion of the ramp, sending out sparks. The smaller figure pointed and said something Kashatok couldn't make out over the roar.

Kashatok stomped into their field of vision. "What in the name of *Ellam Cua* is going on here? We need to get off this station."

Gassy switched off the torch, throwing the cargo bay into sudden, echoing silence. He lifted his visor to reveal his craggy copper face and iron-gray beard. "Glad you're here, captain. Can you climb up there and steady the alignment spanner while I adjust this coupler lock?"

"Me?" Kashatok grit his teeth. Gassy had been trying his best for years to turn Kashatok into an engineer. "Why do you think I hired a mechanic? Is he not qualified?"

Gassy's face flushed blue-green. "Joey's the one who noticed the coupler was loose, so don't you be firing him. I'm the engineer. It's my responsibility." The lines in his face deepened into a scowl. "Just go back to your bottle. I'll comm you when we're done." Slamming his visor back down over his face, Gassy limped back to the coupler and resumed welding.

Feeling a little stung by Gassy's dismissal, Kashatok turned to the kid. Gassy'd been with him a long time. He was the only one who knew the real reason Kashatok'd joined the cartel. The one person the captain actually attempted to please.

"Can I talk to you a sec in private, captain?" Joey chewed one corner of his bottom lip, his brows drawn tightly together. There was a smudge of grease on one cheek, and Kashatok had to resist the urge to reach out and wipe it away.

What the hell is wrong with me? Regretting leaving his rum bottle behind on his desk, he waved a hand for Joey to follow. He stalked across the cargo bay, stopping on the other side of the escape pods. Joey had to jog to catch up, his curly dark hair bobbing in the dirty light. Kashatok put his hands on his hips and forced himself to frown. "Well?"

"Did you notice his foot?"

The question caught Kashatok off guard. He dropped his hands. "What about it?"

"He tried to walk up the wall as if he was wearing grav-boots. He fell pretty hard." Joey shook his head, a furrow between his brows. "He's claiming to have superpowers."

"He does. Usually." Kashatok stepped out from behind the pods so he could see his old engineer. "Is he okay?"

Joey blinked, looking confused. "I think so. But I'm afraid he's going to try it again."

Satisfied his old engineer was indeed all right, he turned back to Joey. "Gassy's getting on in years, which is why I hired a mechanic in the first place."

Joey looked away, face turning a luscious shade of pink. "I'd go up there, but the grav-boots don't fit me. Gassy tried to put them on, but they didn't fit him, either."

Kashatok licked his lips, wondering why he was noticing such minor details about this kid. Why he so badly wanted to make everything all right. It had to be his concern for Gassy bleeding over. Or maybe he'd reached an age where he needed to find a protégé. "We'll get you a pair of grav-boots at the next port." His elbow brushed Joey's arm on his way back toward the dangling ramp, tingling through his nerves clear into his chest. *Damn, I need a drink.* "I'll help Gassy out this time. We're going to miss our opportunity if we don't get going soon."

Joey nodded, scurrying beside Kashatok to keep up. "Yes, sir."

"But I want you to stick close to him and call me if he has trouble again."

"Yes, sir."

Gassy lifted his visor at their approach, one eyebrow raised. He pursed his lips and examined Joey a fraction longer than Kashatok liked.

Kashatok picked up the alignment spanner, feeling oddly defensive. "You can't expect the kid to do everything you can do."

"Never said I did," the old man replied.

"I'll get Joey some grav-boots at the next stop. But I can help you right now so we can get out of here before Syndicorp arrives."

"Sure." Gassy lowered his visor again. "Hop on up there and we'll get it done."

Joey picked up his own visor but didn't put it on, watching Kashatok instead. The kid's gaze made the captain want to hold his spine a little straighter. Kashatok summoned his ionic power and leaped to the top edge of the suspended ramp with one graceful bound. For a moment, he balanced on one foot along the narrow upper edge of metal, acutely aware of Joey's increased heart rate even at this distance.

The visor fell from the kid's fingers, and his brown eyes went wide. "You actually *do* have superpowers?"

"Ionic powers. I told you." Gassy tilted his head. "Stop showing off, captain, and hold that spanner steady."

Kashatok did as requested, and soon the coupler was back in place and the ramp reattached. When he returned to the bridge for liftoff, his steps felt lighter than they had in a very long time. Maybe he'd take the kid under his wing after all.

CHAPTER FOUR

For this final leg of the journey, Kashatok planned to come out almost on top of the freighter. The denaidan crewmen were using their ionic shields instead of nav-grav seats, standing battle-ready in front of the cargo bay door. Kashatok strapped a second sidearm to his belt, watching Chignik and Ekwok do the same. Normally, he'd man the bridge while his men handled boarding, but today he relished the diversion. What was it about the new crewman he found so distracting? His mutinous pet seemed infatuated, too, and was sitting on Joey's shoulder in the nav-grav seat right now. *Just wait until the kid grows some whiskers, then he'll be as distasteful as the rest of the crew.* Yet somehow Kashatok doubted that.

The familiar, slightly nauseating sensation of the ship exiting burn raced through his veins. Aleknagik's voice came over the comm. "Sensor range in sixty. Venting cargo bay now."

Kashatok took a final breath before strengthening his shield against the vacuum of space. Chignik's multiple braids whipped and coiled like live snakes in the hurricane of depressurization. The denaidan ability to withstand vacuum gave them a strong edge when it came to hijacking ships; no waiting to synchronize the ship's atmospheric shielding.

The deck shuddered, and Aleknagik's voice vibrated in his cochlear implant. "Captain, we're taking fire. Brace for evasive maneuvers."

Scowling, Kashatok bent his knees slightly. While it wasn't unusual for a freighter to carry light armament, his intel hadn't included information about heavier guns. The ship vibrated again and jerked left. After a few more maneuvers, a hard jolt told him they'd made contact. "Grapplers in place. Captain. They're refusing to evacuate the bay."

Kashatok grunted. The moment his men popped the door, the freighter's cargo bay would lose pressure. The sudden equalization wreaked havoc on living organisms, and he hated dealing with dead bodies. If he could've sighed, he would've. Well, they'd been fairly warned. Crossing the boarding tube, he popped the freighter door's control panel and shoved his palm against the wiring, sending an ionic pulse through the mechanism. Most ships were frightfully unprotected from ionic pulses. The door slid ajar, allowing a mist of air to blow by as the two cabins equalized. Catching Chignik's eye, Kashatok nodded the go-ahead.

His men surged across the boarding tube, weapons drawn.

Inside, the freighter's cargo bay was lined with stacks upon stacks of detention cells.

Kashatok's twin hearts sank. He'd hijacked a fucking prison ship? Painted lines on the floor delineated walkways between the cages and Syndicorp emblems glared from the walls and floor. To prevent breakouts, Syndicorp would run ships carrying convicts under false manifests, but there were usually tells; excess loading of supplies, cargo weights that didn't change between ports. This sector was a long way from Nunam-qa, however, so the possibility of a prison ship hadn't crossed Kashatok's mind. *Because your mind was preoccupied, you stupid shit.* Fuck, he needed a drink.

From behind the bars, humanoid faces stared back at him, arms groping and eyes bulging as their bodies reacted to the reduced pressure. He opened his mouth to order his men to find the controls for life support, but

Chignik was already on it. There was a chance the prisoners would survive. Closing his eyes for a moment, Kashatok was tempted to offer up a prayer to *Ellam Cua*, although he'd stopped believing in any sort of deity long ago. Why hadn't the freighter's captain mentioned the bay was full of prisoners? Or had he told Aleknagik, who then chose not to mention it? Sometimes Kashatok and his first mate didn't see eye-to-eye.

The moment the cargo bay was at full pressure, he opened the interior airlock and strode down the hall toward the bridge. The other cargo holds likely held more people, but he'd leave his men to sort through them. He was going to find the captain and secure the prisoner list. If there were any cartel members on board, he might yet break even on this job. Ransoming a high-ranking cartel member might even make the hijacking worthwhile.

The empty corridors echoed with the wail of sirens. Ahead, a man stepped from a doorway, his pulse rifle aimed in Kashatok's direction. Kashatok threw the full force of his ionic shield in front of him and took the blast without slowing a step. Pulling his own pistol, he blasted the fellow right between the eyes and continued forward.

As expected, access to the bridge was locked. He blasted the interface and shoved his palm against the wiring.

The door hissed and popped open a crack. Heat seared past his cheek as someone inside fired through the opening. Stepping to one side, he pulled the sliding door the rest of the way open. More pulse fire heated the air.

He waited until they paused to let their weapons cool, then hardened his shield and stepped into view. Two human males wearing bandoleers aimed weapons his way. A third had his back toward the door, his pale blue shirt darkened by sweat. Kashatok dodged, sweeping the closer gunman's feet out from under him. Then he dropped the one farther back with a single shot to the chest.

The third man grabbed a nearby pistol and spun to face him. Kashatok fired again. Sparks erupted from the console as the man dove to one side.

The nearby gunman regained his feet and lunged. Kashatok slammed an ionically charged fist into the man's face. The man's eyes rolled up in his head and he toppled backward over the captain's chair.

Spinning, Kashatok caught a searing blast across his shoulder from the man in the blue shirt, who dodged into the corridor. Ignoring the pain, Kashatok leaped for the door in time to see Chignik lay the man out with a point-blank shot to the chest. The man's body flew backward and landed spread-eagle on the floor. The scent of burned flesh filled the hallway.

Chignik hooked a thumb over his shoulder toward the cargo bay. "Captain, you're not going to like this."

"There's not a single thing I *do* like about this," Kashatok replied, pressing a hand against the burn on his shoulder. His fingers came away sticky with turquoise blood. "Ruined my lucky shirt."

"There's kids on board."

The words stopped Kashatok cold. His frustration at this being a prison ship transformed into revulsion. No one sent kids to Nunam-qa, not even the corp. Kids on board only meant one thing. "Slavers."

Chignik nodded. "Looks like it."

"*Uminaq!*" Kashatok looked at the splayed man with disgust. He wore combat pants tucked into the tops of his boots, but his blue shirt was definitely not military or even prison-issued. The pulse pistol lying a few feet away was also not standard-issue. Kashatok swore again.

Back on the freighter's bridge, the first gunman was dead, but the one he'd punched was still breathing. "Tie him up," Kashatok ordered. "Then release the slaves. I'll be on the *Kinship* trying to salvage some of this mess."

"Aye-aye, Captain."

Kashatok strode back through the cargo bay and across the boarding platform, trying not to think about the bottle of rum in his quarters. These slaves were going to need assistance, and his men weren't going to be happy there was no profit in this hijacking. He hoped at least one of the slaves could fly the damned freighter.

Joy joined the rest of the crew at the big U-shaped table in the galley, her camera taking in each face in turn. While she'd been relieved to be spared the fighting, she'd quickly realized it would be impossible to gather footage while Gassy had her adjusting valves in the jungle. She lingered her recording on Kashatok's wide-shouldered frame. One shoulder of his shirt was torn and stained dark turquoise down one arm, which she could only assume was his blood. This story was going to pack a wallop once she'd put it all together. She not only had pirates and gunfights, but slave traders. *All I need now is a love story to round things off*, she joked to herself. Not that there was much love to be felt in the room at the moment.

Across the table, Cooper dragged a hand over his bald

head, his dark eyes nearly buried in his scowl. "How the fuck'd this happen?"

"Bad intel." Kashatok set his rum down and placed both palms on the table. "However, as your captain, I take full responsibility. Next job, I'll relinquish my shares to make up for it."

"After we stock up on rum." Gassy smirked and gave Joy a wink. He passed a second bottle of rum in her direction.

No one else chuckled, and the scowl on Kashatok's face made Joy think baiting him wasn't a good idea. She pretended to take a sip and passed the bottle on.

The other human, Moore, licked his lips. "They were probably destined for some sex planet. Enayshu Five pays top credits for kids."

Joy cringed. Slaves were bad enough. Child sex slaves? What the hell had she gotten into?

"How many slaves are there?" Manopup's upper tentacles writhed. "I know a man on Orlenny who may be able to unload a few of the males at the beryllium mines."

Kashatok bared his teeth. "We don't deal in slaves."

"You're not going to sell them?" Joy blurted. The black market still traded sentient life, especially outside of Syndicorp space, so she'd assumed that's what would happen.

"No live cargo." Kashatok spoke through gritted teeth.

Gassy laughed and pointed at Jhikik pacing the back of the captain's chair. "Not since that shipment of exotic pets ran amok."

Joy affected a scowl. While the little netorpok'd been a pleasant companion, she was concerned his affection would give her away. She'd already had to shoo the little creature off twice since sitting down at the galley table. "What'll happen to the slaves, then?"

"Not our problem," Aleknagik said.

Kashatok added, "Doc's over there now, sorting out the casualties."

Joy re-counted the crew, realizing one of the denaidans was missing. She hadn't exactly been formally introduced to them, and keeping track of the odd names had been difficult. The crew seemed polarized, with the denaidans turning to Gassy and the other men turning to Aleknagik. Like planets around a sun, they all maintained a respectful distance from their captain.

"Fucking waste of our medical supplies, you ask me," Cooper grumbled, with Moore nodding in agreement.

"I have some added bad news." Aleknagik waved away the rum as it came in his direction. "We took light damage from their guns during our approach. Long range sensors are down."

Leaning back in his chair, Kashatok sighed. "I also damaged the freighter's bridge with my pulse pistol during the fight. It'll need repairs. No sense rescuing them, only to let them sit here and rot in space."

Joy's assessment of the captain shifted once again. Sexy. Mysterious. And now, altruistic. *Like some kind of Robin Hood.* He was totally going to smash her female demographic. She zoomed her camera in on his face once more and panned down his chest to where his fingers toyed with Jhikik's tail. What would those fingertips feel like tracing across her skin? She shook her head to clear it. Yep, going to smash 'em.

Gassy grunted. "Joey can handle the freighter's bridge repairs while I go outside and have a look at our sensors."

"You sure, Gassy?" The denaidan with a buff-colored beard asked. "I could take a camera out for you."

Gassy scowled at him. "Don't be treating me like an invalid, Ekwok."

"Just trying to help." Ekwok held up both hands defensively and turned to a denaidan with elaborately braided beard and hair. "You find someone on board able to navigate?"

"A few seem capable. I'm more worried about them maintaining their systems until they come up with a safe place to go."

Cooper crossed his big arms and scowled around the table. "I can't believe we're just handing a perfectly good freighter over to a bunch of slaves."

Aleknagik sprawled back in his chair and cut a sideways look at the captain. "I wonder, as well."

Kashatok rose slowly, his presence suddenly filling the entire room. "You want to argue with me?" Edgy silence filled the galley. "As soon as they're on their way, I'll have a new job lined up." Joy's heart nearly leaped out of her body as he leaned toward her. "I want you to pull up any corp' information you can find on their system while you're over there fixing their bridge."

She cleared her throat, feeling light-headed under his smoldering gaze. "Syndicorp information? But they're not a corp' ship."

"Don't fool yourself, kid." Kashatok broke eye contact and swept his bottle to his lips for a long swallow. "Syndicorp turns a blind eye to its subsidiaries as long as they're turning a profit."

She'd eavesdropped on enough of her mother's conversations to know the corporation didn't always play aboveboard, but slavery? No way. Still, she didn't want Kashatok's anger directed her way. "Aye-aye, sir. I'll run a check."

Kashatok lowered one arm to allow Jhikik to scurry up his shoulder. "I don't want to spend a lot of time here, everyone, so get your jobs done and let's burn out of here. I'll be in my cabin."

Joy rose with the rest, declining another sip of the shared rum, and headed to the freighter with her tool kit. Anything she could do to stay off the captain's radar was fine by her.

She crossed the boarding tube, camera taking in everything as she entered the other ship's bay. After hearing the crew talk about the decompression, she'd tried to prepare herself for what lay ahead; the reality turned out much worse than she expected. Rows of corpses lay on the floor, and the stench of unwashed bodies clogged her throat. How long had these people lived in these small cages? At the end of the huge bay, the tall, copper-skinned denaidan doctor was administering oxygen to one girl, while a man cradled a limp child nearby. A wailing woman knelt a few bodies over. Others walked among the rows, obviously searching for loved ones.

Joy steeled her spine and turned her focus toward the corridor to the bridge. Footage be damned; if she looked any more, she'd lose it. The air reeked of devastation and heartbreak. *Do not, under any circumstances, cry.* She marched with heavy footsteps, holding her breath as long as possible across the cargo bay.

Reaching the bridge, she found two men and a woman already had a damaged console pulled apart. The discolored panels and melted wiring lay scattered on the floor. She cringed. She wasn't completely familiar with the freighter's systems, and now she didn't even have a baseline for how it had looked put together to begin with. Sighing, she showed one of the ex-slaves how to reroute the main interface, then checked on the other systems.

After sending two ex-slaves off to readjust the life support, she plugged a data cube into the system and set up parameters to look for anything related to Syndicorp. The freighter had been destined for a stop in the rakwiji-controlled Onskzu system. She shuddered, imagining the horrible things planned for slaves owned by rakwiji. Another stop was scheduled at a Syndicorp aligned planet in the Pulati system. She double checked, frowning. The freighter had valid planetary access codes.

Fuck.

The captain was right. Someone inside Syndicorp must be running slaves. Mother was going to be pissed. On the other hand, this might be an even bigger story than an exposé on pirates. Joy settled in to download the slave ship's files. After she finished with these pirates, she was going to track down the Syndicorp slavers and blow the lid off their operation.

CHAPTER FIVE

Kashatok's men were discontent now, and rightfully so. Hell, he was pissed, too. This entire effort had been money and time down the drain. He swiped past cartel information that was already outdated because of his careless selection. Even a relatively wealthy fleet ship like his existed on a job-to-job basis, and what he didn't invest in fuel and supplies, he spent on rum. His men had nothing to spare, either. Between gambling and drinking, his denaidan crew always came back penniless, while the posungi and the humans understandably spent most of their time and money at a brothel.

Looking up from his review of manifests and shipping routes, he rubbed his lips. What would Joey choose to do once he was awarded a share?

Realizing he was daydreaming, he resumed his search for a new target. While he didn't mind ransoming an odd prisoner or two, selling innocents into slavery was a completely different level of piracy in Kashatok's view. He avoided passenger or colonist ships for a reason; he didn't want to offer his men the option of making money selling slaves. If he let that happen, they'd be raping and pillaging people's homesteads.

His desk interface flashed as the ship's warning lights went on.

"Captain," Aleknagik's voice came over the comm. "The freighter must've gotten off a distress call. We have troopers on short-range scanners. They'll be in range in less than five."

"*Uminaq.*" Kashatok shot to his feet, sending Jhikik scurrying away. "Disconnect and ready us for burn."

"Doc and the new kid are still on the freighter."

"Tell them to get their asses back on board."

"I already told the doc through his implant. But I can't reach the kid."

Kashatok swore again, striding to the door. The *Kinship* came first—his crew knew that—but he'd sent Joey to go fix the freighter. It was Kashatok's responsibility to make sure he made it back aboard. "Hold position until I tell you to break."

"Aye-aye."

Racing to the cargo hold, Kashatok covered the boarding platform in two bounding strides and headed for the freighter's bridge.

A scrawny slave blocked the corridor, eyes wide beneath his bushy brows. "Is something wrong?"

"Troopers." Kashatok shoved past him toward the bridge. "If you want to hang onto this ship, I suggest you get this ship operational and fly your asses out of here."

Aleknagik's voice vibrated in his cochlear implant. "We're taking fire, Captain."

"I'm on the freighter. Hold until my say so." He dashed the last few steps to the bridge.

Joey looked up at him from the freighter's comm seat. "Captain?"

"Come on." He held out a hand.

"Uh, okay." The kid licked his lips and looked around. "Let me gather my things."

"No time." He grabbed Joey's arm and all but dragged

him past the gawking slaves. The ship shuddered and alarms wailed in protest.

He picked up his pace, but Joey's shorter legs were no match for his ionically-enhanced strides. Barely pausing his steps, he swept the kid up across his shoulders, wincing as his wounded arm took the weight, and ran for the boarding platform. Ahead, the airlock to the cargo door stood partway closed, a canister lodged between the panels. Air rushed past him toward the gap. *Great Ellam Cua, the boarding tube was compromised?*

The airlock behind him clanged shut.

Debris-filled air rushed around him, emptying from the nearby compartments. On instinct, he brought up his ionic shield, shutting out the impending vacuum. Joey's weight wriggled against his neck. He couldn't extend his shield over the kid in this position. Setting Joey down, Kashatok shouted over the roar of evacuating air. "Climb on my back and don't let go!"

Joey hunched against the insistent pull of the wind and mounted up without any further encouragement. Wrapping his legs around Kashatok's waist, he pressed his chest against Kashatok's back. The unmistakable sensation of breasts met Kashatok's shoulder blades. *What the hell?*

But there was no time to think on that now. The air would be gone in moments. Kashatok drew hard on his power, shrouding Joey along with himself. He couldn't maintain the extended shield for long, but the boarding platform was only a handful of strides away.

He shoved the blocked airlock open wide enough to allow him to pass. The cargo bay on the other side was already empty of anything and anyone not locked down. Through the gaping maw of the cargo hatch, he could see the *Kinship* drifting away. *Uminaq!*

Aided by the last of the escaping air, he bounded across the floor and leaped out the open hatch toward the boarding platform. Joey's cheek pressed hard against his shoulder, limbs like trembling bands of iron around Kashatok's hips and shoulders. On all sides, lifeless slaves spun in a slow-motion dance, following the slow wake of the *Kinship's* departure.

Framed in the light from the open boarding hatch, Aleknagik stood with one hand poised on the boarding tube control. The atmospheric retention shield flickered to life over the opening. The tube continued to retract. Kashatok strained forward, but even his ionic power could do nothing except hold back the vacuum. All he had was his momentum to catch the ship.

He reached the narrowing opening moments before the hatch shuddered to a close, pulling himself and Joey over the lip and into the cargo bay. Rolling across the deck, he circled both arms to protect Joey's head. He came to a stop poised on both elbows, looking down into very feminine, liquid brown eyes.

For the first time in over a decade, he thought of Aiyana. Remembered her dual, racing heartbeats in the final throes of passion. A giddy, anxious rhythm not unlike this woman's now.

He lurched to his feet, wrenching himself away from the bittersweet memory.

And from the desire to do it again.

Clinging to Kashatok's back through the empty weightlessness of space without a suit—and surviving— had been more than Joy could process. Now he leaned over her, breath caressing her face. She was paralyzed. Exhilarated.

Kashatok stared at her as if she'd slapped him, then rose to his feet without a word and faced his first mate. "You fucking pulled the boarding tube."

Joy rolled to her knees, heart racing with adrenaline. A hard jolt nearly flattened her against the deck.

Aleknagik held up both hands. "We're taking fire." The deck shuddered as if to prove his point. "I couldn't hold the door forever, not if we expect to raise our shields and hit burn before they blow us up. Besides, you made the jump."

The lights flickered, and alarms began to sound. The comm crackled. "Direct hit! Burn drive is offline!"

"Fuuuck!" Kashatok stumbled to the nearby console.

Joy's racing heart skidded to a panicked halt. No burn drive? And they were under attack? She struggled to her feet. Gassy would need her help.

Kashatok shouted into the comm. "Gassy, can you get us up and running?"

Silence.

Kashatok repeated, "Gassy, report."

Joy bent her knees, trying to remain upright on the shuddering deck, and aimed herself toward the door to engineering.

"Aleknagik, get your ass to the bridge and pilot us out of here," Kashatok ordered behind her. "I'll help Gassy."

The first mate darted past her without a hitch in his stride, apparently not walking on the same ship she was on. Then a huge hand all but lifted her by the scruff of her tunic. "You. To a nav-grav seat."

She kicked her legs, pedaling along helplessly. "But—"

"No buts. I don't know what your game is or why you're on my ship, but until we hit the next port, you're to stay in your quarters."

He knew. Holy hell, he knew she was a woman. Well, of course he would. Every inch of her had been locked against him during the jump back to the ship. There was no way he didn't notice her softness against his broad, hard back. Yet surely he wasn't going to relegate her to quarters now? "But Gassy may need my help."

He growled—actually growled—a low sound that carried up his arm and into her bones where he held the collar of her shirt. "This ship is no place for a woman."

Half-carrying, half dragging her, Kashatok propelled her toward the area behind the bridge with the nav-grav seats, the deck rocking and swaying beneath them. As they passed the open door to engineering, the scent of melted conduit and burning hair wafted out.

Kashatok released his hold on her tunic and took a step inside the doorway. "Gassy?!"

Steam and coolant misted from the room, but Joy spotted the engineer in the jungle, wedged between two mangled pipes. She pointed. "There!"

Ducking past Kashatok, she wove between the pipes and edged past an arc of scalding spray to reach the shutoff valves. Everything was coated in boiling coolant. She grabbed hold of the scalding metal and twisted, ignoring the heat against her palms. The spray slowed to a trickle.

Turning, she found Kashatok lowering the engineer's motionless body to the floor. "Gassy, can you hear me?"

The old man still breathed but remained unconscious. Ugly welts covered his skin, and part of his hair had been scalded away.

Joy backed toward the door. "I'll get the doc."

"No." Kashatok lifted the big engineer as if he weighed nothing. The ship jerked and shuddered. "Stay here and see what you can do to get us out of here. I'll take him to medical." His gaze cut into her like a welding laser. "When I get back, I expect some answers."

Part of her smirked, but now was not the time to gloat about him needing her skills. The ship shuddered with another impact. She was on a pirate ship, and they were under attack.

Swearing in every language she knew, she got to work on the diagnostics, only half aware that she'd forgotten to turn on her camera.

Kashatok lay Gassy on the exam table and held up a hand as his medic began to ask questions. "Just take care of him."

Doc pressed his copper-toned lips into a thin line and turned to search his cabinets.

Without time to dwell on the fate of one man, Kashatok dashed from the medical bay. The entire ship was about to be blown to bits. He burst onto the bridge, taking in the massive trooper frigate filling the rear view screen. "Update," he commanded.

"Our sensors are still offline," Aleknagik ground out from the pilot's seat, his shoulders rigid while he worked the controls. "Continuing evasive maneuvers."

Cooper called over his shoulder from munitions, "Starboard guns are down."

"Rear shields at half strength," Ekwok reported.

Bracing his legs as the deck rocked under another impact, Kashatok scanned the internal diagnostic over his starboard gunner's shoulder. The *Kinship* wasn't heavily armed to begin with, relying more on speed and surprise. He watched the shield rating tick down another notch.

He glanced back at the forward view screen. "How far are we from the mining belt?"

"Just under point-one parsec," Chignik said.

"Aleknagik, help Ekwok with shields." Kashatok moved to the co-pilot seat on Aleknagik's right. "I'll take the helm."

As he splayed his fingers over the controls, Kashatok gauged the cloud of rocky debris on the view screen. The system had been mined for generations, creating a belt of dust that smugglers used for rendezvous. He swung them toward the nearby spray of asteroids, taking in trajectories and clearances with an intuition built on years of piloting the *Kinship*. Even so, maneuvering without the use of sensors was going to push his limits.

"Captain, you certain that's wise at this speed?" Aleknagik's hands lingered over the pilot controls.

Kashatok wasn't sure, but he preferred random asteroid dust over the torpedoes that were targeting the *Kinship's* weak spots. With any luck, the asteroid particles would interfere with the frigate's targeting system. He bared his teeth and pushed the thrusters to maximum. "Direct all power to shields. If we can't run, we'll hide."

The view screen lit up from the impact of a small asteroid as Kashatok dodged an L-shaped chunk of rock twice the size of the *Kinship's* cargo bay. He spun the ship on its axis, slipping between a rotating trio of asteroids. The hull rattled and pinged with small impacts. Another torpedo slammed into them from behind.

"Shields at twenty percent, captain!" Ekwok cried out.

"Redirect power from life support if you have to!" Kashatok glanced at his aft view screen. "Just keep up those shields!"

The pursuing ship had slowed, too large to dodge between asteroids, and was now pacing the edge of the field. More rocks exploded into glittering mist in the *Kinship's* wake as the frigate continued firing. *Let them see through that,* Kashatok thought.

Coming up on a particularly large asteroid, Kashatok dropped the ship into a nosedive. The dark, pitted surface loomed in his view screen. He thought he heard someone groan just before he pulled up, leveling out along the uneven surface. The *Kinship* bucked and jerked. He reigned in his throttle, coming to a full stop next to a jutting column of rock and ice. The ship slammed into the protrusion and rocks cascaded over the hull, bouncing and sailing into each other in a veil of floating debris.

He cut power to the thrusters and shouted into the comm, "Power down all systems!"

The bridge went silent. One by one, the consoles and lights flickered off, leaving only the dull yellow of a single emergency backup. For a few breathless moments, they all sat there staring through the limited angle on the view screen while the asteroid they rested upon rotated them into the frigate's line of sight.

Impacts still blossomed throughout the asteroid field, shattering rock and ice. A blast landed nearby on the asteroid's surface, but it was only one of many hitting the surrounding debris. The weapons fire shifted farther away, leaving behind jagged, gyrating hunks of rock. Their asteroid rotated them out of sight.

Back into sight.

The torpedo fire tapered to almost nothing.

After a few moments, Aleknagik spoke softly. "I think they lost us."

"Maintain full silence," Kashatok ordered. *Let them think we're part of the debris.*

No one dared breathe for long moments.

The frigate's fire ceased. For a while, it paced within range of their view screen. Finally, it moved back in the direction they'd come.

"Long-range scanners are still down," Chignik whispered, as if afraid the frigate might hear him.

Kashatok asked, "How long can we sit here without life support?"

"Humans got a couple of hours," Ekwok replied.

"All right." Kashatok rolled his shoulders, looking around at his men. "Cooper, Moore, hit your bunks. I don't want you using up any more oxygen than you need to. We'll sit here awhile and hope they don't come back. We need time to repair our burn drive, anyway." He took a deep breath. "Just so you all know, Gassy's been injured. It doesn't look good."

Ekwok and Chignik hung their heads. Cooper let out a string of curses.

"Aleknagik, you have the bridge." Kashatok headed for the door. "I'll be in engineering with… the kid." Damn, he had a female on board. Worse yet, he couldn't just confine her to quarters. Without Gassy, he needed her. How could this have happened? His gut churned. Women were not meant for this kind of stress. Hell, he wasn't meant for this kind of stress.

She put herself in this position, he thought.

But that didn't really make him feel any better.

Chapter Six

Joy put all her weight against the wrench and pushed. The floor was still slippery with coolant, and her feet scrabbled for purchase. She couldn't determine what was wrong until she got the coolant flowing again, and she could barely see to work under engineering's single emergency light. And this bolt refused to budge. If she couldn't prove herself useful, she worried what Kashatok might do. But she was fairly certain she wouldn't be tossed out an airlock, at least. He'd surprised her with his weird, chivalric—or was it chauvinistic?—demand she go sit in a nav-grav seat. It felt like he was trying to protect her. A gentleman rogue. Maybe that's what she would title her exposé… If she could convince him to keep her on board.

She threw her weight forward again, swearing as her feet went out from under her.

Two powerful hands gripped her waist, holding her upright.

She stiffened, skin tingling. Turning slowly, the warm, masculine scent of sweet rum hit her senses. Kashatok stared down at her, face darkened by shadow. "Why are you on board my ship?"

She licked her lips, unable to speak or look away. What had she been thinking? He wasn't gentlemanly at all. He oozed danger.

He stepped closer, forcing her back against the tangle of pipes, stopping with the entire length of his body pressed against hers. "Do you have any idea what I could do to you… what my men could do to you if they find out?"

His breath fanned her face. Damn, he smelled great. Her heart threatened to burst from her chest. But she knew there was only one way to handle a bully. Lifting her chin, she said, "So don't tell them."

His nostrils flared and she could feel his muscles tense against her as if he was on the edge of restraint. He stared down into her face for a long moment. When he spoke, his deep voice felt strangely intimate in the silent engineering bay. "You don't know what you're asking."

She barely dared to breathe. He was close enough to kiss, and she wasn't sure whether she should be terrified or excited. Her nipples hardened against his chest. She steeled herself, trying to make her voice authoritative. "What I do know is you need the burn drive fixed. And Gassy's probably in no shape to do it."

Without warning, he stepped backward.

It was all she could do to stop herself from trailing after him like a lamprey on a shark. Here she was getting turned on while he was worried about his engineer. Softening her voice, she asked, "How is he?"

He shook his head, his dark eyes pinched. "Doc's doing what he can."

Her chest tightened. Gassy had been so good to her. Inviting her to cards. Standing up for her with the captain. What would she do without his mentoring? "Anything I can do?"

"Get the drive fixed," Kashatok said through clenched teeth.

"I'm trying." She gestured to the pipe behind her. "I can't get this bolt loose. The diagnostics won't work until I replace this valve."

Lifting one arm, he leaned past her, filling her vision with the mouth-watering copper skin above his neckline and the metal bands holding his beard. With one push, the bolt gave with a teeth-grinding squawk. His breath fanned her cheek. "This just proves my point."

Keeping a logical thought in her head was next to impossible with him so near. *He did that on purpose.* She clutched the baggy sides of her cargo pants to prevent her hands from wrapping around his middle and pulling him even closer. "What point?"

"Women don't belong on my ship."

Well, that ended that moment. She stood taller, temper rising. "That's not fair. You used your superpower, or whatever you call it. You wouldn't have expected Cooper to move a bolt like that."

His features remained hard.

"Fuck you, then. Fix it yourself. I'll go back to my bunk." She placed both hands against his chest and shoved. A shock like a static electric discharge tingled up her arms, but he didn't budge.

He stared down at her for a long moment. A vein on his forehead pulsed. "I can't."

She rolled her eyes. This guy was a tangle of contradictions, strength and vulnerability, sexiness and terrifying anger. She wasn't quite sure what to do with him. "So you do need me?"

His shoulders rose and fell with a breath. Finally, he backed up. "Can you just tell me what to do?"

She moved to the nearby console. "The main flux point's been blown. Start by replacing that valve."

"I meant tell me and then go to your bunk."

"No." She laughed and turned around, resting her bottom against the console. Like she was going to let him hide her away and take all the credit. "I won't know each step until we fix the previous one and run a new diagnostic."

He sighed. "Can you handle it alone?"

Her shoulders sagged. "I'm a shuttle mechanic, not a ship engineer. K-class vessels are complex. I'm going to need help from someone who knows this ship."

Covering his eyes with one hand, he squeezed his temples, then ran his fingers down his face and beard. "Fine. What do we do next?"

She was proud of herself for resisting a grin as she moved toward the cabinets where Gassy kept spare parts. She was going to work the captain like a dog.

And get a ton of footage while she was at it.

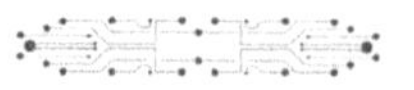

Joy removed the tertiary coil matrix and pulled aside all the conduits to the lateral thrusters before shimmying herself into the tight space in the bowels of the main drive. She stared at the fused electronics inside the frequency inverter. How was she supposed to fix that? She couldn't repair a frequency inverter. The part was a specialty instrument that required calibration both before and after installation. Without the frequency inverter, they had no burn drive, and without a burn drive, they had only thrusters to get them out of here.

So much for proving herself useful.

Holy hell, what was she going to do? She wriggled out of the narrow space, swearing at the baggy pocket of her cargo pants as it tore on a protruding bolt. What were they going to do? She could always call her mother. Yet after what Kashatok had just put them through to escape the troopers, she had a feeling that calling on Syndicorp for help would not only ruin her exposé, it would probably end with these men's executions. Kashatok might be a pirate, but he didn't deserve the death penalty.

The captain entered engineering as she emerged from the jungle carrying a heavy toolbox in one hand. He leaned forward and took the handle from her. Her heartbeat thrilled as his skin brushed hers. Since discovering she was a woman, he'd avoided getting within touching distance, which for some reason made stupid moments like this more exciting.

"What's wrong?" he asked.

Her face heated, and it took her a moment to remember her task at hand. "How far is the nearest space station?"

Kashatok's forehead drew into a frown. "Maybe half a parsec? Why?"

Jhikik took the opportunity to scramble down Kashatok's front, using his long beard as a rope, and reached for her. She accepted him without thinking, distracting herself by petting his soft fur. She wasn't a navigator, but she knew parsecs were usually measured by burn cycles. How long would it take to travel half a parsec using only thrusters? Probably a really long time.

She swallowed. Now that she couldn't fix the drive, would he relegate her to quarters? She didn't like the idea of being trapped in that storeroom for months while the ship limped back to civilization. She chewed her bottom lip, seeking any last-ditch alternatives. "Is Gassy awake yet?"

"Sort of. Doc says he's doing better." Worry still filled Kashatok's eyes.

Joy gulped. Poor Gassy. "Can I see him?"

Kashatok nodded, and in silence, they headed to the medical bay, Kashatok's long strides keeping him well ahead of her.

Gassy lay inside a shimmering sterility chamber on one bed, huge blisters covering most of his skin. Despite the guilt churning through her gut, she turned on her camera. Gritty footage brought ratings, and that's why she was here, right? She hung back as Kashatok approached his bedside and zoomed in on Kashatok's face.

"How're you doing, old man?" asked Kashatok.

The engineer cracked open one eye—literally cracked, the crusted blister making an audible sound as the lid lifted. His other eye remained swelled shut. "I'll snap out of this in no time." His voice sounded like rocks grating against each other. He caught sight of her and one corner of his blistered lips turned up in what might've been an attempt at a smile. "Hey, you. Got my baby up and running yet?"

Joy stepped forward and tried to smile encouragingly. "You don't happen to have a spare frequency inverter hidden away, do you? Or know how to fix one?"

His already horrific-looking face crumpled. The flashing lights tracking his vitals flickered red. "That part's beyond a ship engineer's skills."

Well, at least that made her feel a little less inadequate. But it still didn't solve the issue of being stuck on board this vessel for weeks, maybe months, while they languished in dead space.

"So now what?" Kashatok kept his gaze on the injured man.

Gassy fumbled for a tube of water next to him, taking a moment to pull it toward his lips. Joy yearned to help him, but wouldn't dare breach the sterility chamber. When he'd finished, he said, "Put out a distress call."

Kashatok squeezed his eyes shut. "It could take weeks for a distress call to reach someone in the fleet."

"Last I heard, the *Hardship* was running this quadrant. They may be close by." Gassy's one good eye glinted with something Joy couldn't quite decipher.

Kashatok's skin flushed blue-green, and Joy realized for the first time that denaidans blushed green. Kinda cute. Then Kashatok's upper lip broadened into a sneer. Not so cute. He looked at Joy, his gaze traveling from her face to her breasts, then he narrowed his eyes and turned back to his engineer. "What are you saying?"

Something inside Joy's gut twisted, and she glanced down at her chest, half expecting her boobs to be hanging out. Nope, still well covered by her baggy shirt.

Gassy answered, "C'mon, Kashatok. You must know. I figured it out right after the first burn when Jhikik wouldn't leave her side."

Joy's breath caught in her throat. Had he just said 'her?'

Gassy knew?

"Uminaq." Kashatok fisted his hands at his sides, refusing to look at the female beside him. He'd been in her presence for a day and a half now, feasting his eyes on her every move and forcing himself to keep his distance. And here Gassy'd known all along? Kashatok'd never needed a drink more than he did right now. "And you didn't think to say anything?"

"So you could do what?" Gassy's voice creaked, and he reached for the tube of water again. "We were already headed to the job. And she's a damned good mechanic. I needed her help."

Kashatok flared his nostrils. If the old man hadn't been critically injured, Kashatok might've considered slugging him. "We burned past at least three inhabited worlds. It would've taken us no time to drop her off."

"She got you to come out of your damned cabin. First time I've played cards with you in years. It's good to see you paying attention to something besides rum." Gassy chuckled, which transformed into a horrible wet cough. "She's fitting in fine. Give her a chance."

Kashatok threw both hands up, chest blazing with anger. "A chance at what? A life of danger? A pirate ship's no place for a woman."

Gassy spoke softly. "With the nanites, we may not always be pirates."

Not be a pirate? The fire inside of Kashatok went out as if all the room's oxygen had been sucked away. He'd left his planet at sixteen, and was fast approaching the day he could say he'd spent more days on a ship than he had on land. If he wasn't a pirate, what else was there? Yet he couldn't stop his gaze from drifting to the dark-haired woman at the foot of Gassy's bed. He'd found her intriguing even before discovering she was female. How long had it been since he'd craved company of any sort? *Ellam Cua*, he wanted her as much as he'd ever wanted anyone or anything. And that only made him more dangerous. "You believe that corp' bullshit? Their technology is the reason denaidans need something like the nanites in the first place. Anyway, you know that can't help me."

The female's brows were drawn together. "What kind of nanites are you guys talking about?"

Gassy ignored her. "I know you believe you can't be around women, but I've always said your story has some holes. And consider this—she needs the nanites for her own safety. We can't risk anything happening to her. She's the only one who can get this ship up and running."

The female placed her hands on her hips. "*I* need them? Kashatok, what's he talking about?"

Kashatok refused to look at her, his eyes instead focusing on Gassy's brittle looking skin. "*You're* my engineer, old man."

Gassy lay back against the pillows. "I won't be returning to engineering anytime soon, and you know it. Go make that distress call. Then I suggest you educate your new ship engineer about denaidan birds and bees. I'm going to take a short nap now."

Hearts thundering, Kashatok stood there a moment, staring down at the closest thing to a mentor—maybe even a father—he had. Gassy's assumptions about the female both grated on Kashatok and nurtured a seed of hope; the engineer really believed in the nanite's potential. Even for a man who'd caused his lover's death.

Shaking his head, Kashatok looked away. Gassy was wrong. Aiyana had died in Kashatok's arms. The female was not safe with him, and the nanites wouldn't change that. Yet he didn't trust that she was safe anywhere on this ship, either, not with the way the men joked about females. Impossible as it seemed, he'd have to keep her close and keep himself under control.

Reaching out, he grasped her arm, fingers easily encircling her biceps. "Until we reach port, you're not to be out of my sight."

"What? Why?" Her flesh trembled beneath his fingers, but she didn't try to pull away. "Are you going to tell me what's going on?"

He propelled her toward the door and into the corridor. The physical connection with her arm thrummed through his senses as if her very blood flowed into his veins. *Anaq,* he wanted rum. But there'd be no escape to the bottle for him, not as long as she was on his ship.

She hurried beside him, breathing hard. "Are you going to tell me what this is all about?"

He turned toward his cabin, praying they didn't run into anyone along the way. He never invited anyone into his cabin, and if the men saw Joey enter, they'd know something was up. *If they don't know already.* Gassy had known and not said a word.

The corridor remained blessedly empty. He pushed her inside ahead of him, closing the door behind them. Alone with her, he realized just how precarious the situation was. Every flutter of her heartbeat brushed his senses like a seductress's caress, and he couldn't seem to drag his gaze away from the kid's... the female's... Joey's?... mouth. "What's your real name?" he demanded.

"Joy." She lifted her chin defiantly. "I never lied to you."

His lip twitched, fighting an involuntary smile. *Cute.* Female or not, she was a little punk. "And why are you on my ship? I specifically told you I forbid females."

Through his heightened senses, he felt Joy's body temperature increase. He saw a light sweat break out on her brow. Jhikik, who'd been quietly nestled against the crook of her neck this entire time, perked up and jumped to the floor. Kashatok ignored his querying chirp, refusing to break his gaze.

The pink tip of her tongue moistened her lips before she bit down on her plump bottom lip. Finally, she breathed out, "Shouldn't you be making that distress call rather than worrying about me?"

Resisting the urge to dip his head and claim her mouth, he frowned more deeply. Unfortunately, she was right. He let out a slow breath. There wasn't time to get into a game of words with her, not while they were hanging on the edge of an asteroid with limited power and a busted burn drive. Pivoting, he marched to his desk comm and coded a distress call on several secure fleet channels. The sooner he could get the ship fixed, the sooner he could rid himself of this distracting female.

Once he'd finished, he looked up to find Joy bent in front of the open door to his hydroponic system. Her loose cargo pants had spread tight across her ass, revealing the roundness of her hips. He felt his cock stir, something that hadn't happened in a long time. *Ellam Cua*, bringing her to his cabin may have been a mistake. He forced his attention to the gleefully chittering netorpok swinging among the branches inside the cage. "I don't let him do that."

She looked over her shoulder, one hand still buried in the innards of the hydroponic control box. "Who?"

"Jhikik. He'll eat every leaf in sight if I let him."

She straightened to watch the netorpok drop from one limb, suspended only by his tail, only to swing onto another branch. "But he seems so happy."

He marched over, reaching past her into the cage door. Jhikik chittered and dodged, but Kashatok caught him by the scruff and dragged him out. The little *tunrak* sunk his tiny teeth into Kashatok's thumb before scurrying away indignantly. Kashatok couldn't blame him, but he couldn't let him have free rein, either. "You know better, Jhik."

Joy's breath brushed his arm. "Be gentle. He's just doing what netorpok do."

As if she knows what netorpok do. Over the subtle perfume of the naujiar flowers behind her, he picked up a scent like sun-warmed citrus coming off her skin. The heady mixture made his mouth water. He forced himself back a step. "Tell me why you're here."

She tilted her head, once again chewing her lip. Her pulse pattered with erratic indecision. Finally, she took a deep breath. "What if I told you I'm filming a documentary?"

It took him a moment to understand what she'd said. Then he laughed. "You're making a movie? Of us?"

"Not a movie. A documentary for RealTime News. I want to show viewers inside the swashbuckling world of black market trading and deep-space piracy—"

"Hold on. You're a reporter?" He hadn't seen that coming. RealTime News was known for sensationalistic reality reporting, but that could be a front. "How do I know you're not a corp' spy?"

She lifted her chin. "You don't. But I'm not."

It wasn't a lie. He could feel it in her heartbeat. In the steadiness of her eye contact.

She continued, "I plan on blowing open that Syndicorp slaving ring after I finish my pirate story."

He narrowed his eyes. "Fixing ships and making news-reels aren't exactly complimentary skill sets. Tell me how that happened."

"I'm not incompetent at either one, if that's what you're implying." Her slender throat rippled as she swallowed.

He took a step forward. She'd basically admitted she wasn't a mechanic. How could she take over Gassy's job? "If you aren't going to be able to handle the repairs, I may as well skip all this self-control bullshit."

She leaned back against the cage wall, her gaze remaining locked with his. Her racing pulse kept time with his own, and her eyes were dilated almost black. "I can fix the ship once I have the part."

He took another step, senses on fire. She smelled so delectably fine, the faint and familiar tang of mechanical grease overridden by warm citrus and naujiar perfume.

"But who needs self-control?" She licked those plump lips.

The move was too much. His mouth was against hers before he knew it. Joy's mouth met his, lips softly parted and ready. She arched her back so her breasts made contact with his chest.

Like awakening from a nightmare, his entire body seemed to recover consciousness. Her lips were like a first taste of a rare drug. The softness of her body against his like the warm kiss of the sun after winter.

She opened to him, melted against him, the tip of her tongue tracing his upper lip. He braced both elbows against the cage on either side of her, molding his body against hers.

Her hands slid around his sides, settling beneath his arms, sending rivers of desire coursing through his newly awakened bloodstream. She tasted as good as she smelled, and he delved into her mouth, snaking one hand to the back of her head to hold her. Her short hair felt like pirelux silk between his fingers.

He shifted, placing one leg between hers. She widened her stance to accommodate him, and the heat from her core radiating against his thigh made him groan. Cock throbbing with desire, he broke the kiss and trailed his mouth along her cheek to below her ear.

She exhaled his name, tilting her head back and wrapping her hands around his shoulder blades to pull him closer.

Her feminine scent was stronger here, enveloping him until only this moment existed. Only Joy existed.

"*Kinship*, this is the *Hardship*." A man's unfamiliar voice caused him to jerk away from her as if he'd been electrocuted. "We've received your distress signal. Please send coordinates to your location."

Chapter Seven

J oy reeled in the aftermath of Kashatok's kiss. Her lips tingled, and her skin craved his nearness and warmth. After telling him she was a reporter, the last thing she'd expected was a kiss, especially a kiss like *that*. Damn. She should've told him the truth a long time ago.

Across the room, the captain had his back to her, shoulders rigid as he brought up a holo image on his desk comm. A copper-skinned face appeared, hovering above the desktop with a shaggy mane of hair rivaling Ekwok's tawny mess and twin-braided beard. Did all denaidans look so barbarically hot?

Kashatok's fingers danced across the desktop controls. "Good to see you, Captain Qaiyaan. Relaying exact coordinates now. Keep an eye out for that trooper vessel."

Qaiyaan's beard swayed as he looked down, presumably at his screens. "Looks like we can reach you in a few hours. We don't have a frequency inverter for a K-class vessel on board, but I think we can figure out how to piggyback your ship to the nearest station for repairs."

The face of a gorgeous human woman with charcoal eyes and dark hair appeared over the other captain's shoulder and whispered something in his ear. Apparently banning women from ships wasn't a denaidan thing or a pirate thing. Did that mean it was personal?

Joy straightened her baggy shirt, watching the familiar way the woman laid her fingertips on the captain's shoulder as she spoke. A strange yearning broke open inside Joy's chest, forcing her to swallow, hard.

The man on the holo nodded, then turned back to the screen. "Captain Kashatok, we're still hoping you can track down information about a secret corp' test lab in this sector. Have you had a chance to look into it?"

Kashatok glanced over his shoulder at Joy. "Now's not a good time, Captain. I'll see what I can pull together before you get here."

"You understand how important this is?" Qaiyaan's eyes glittered with intensity. "That lab may hold the only key to our people's survival."

"I said it's not a good time." Kashatok killed the connection.

Joy frowned at Kashatok's back. "Was that a good idea? We kinda need him to help us."

"He'll come." He continued to stare at the spot the holo image had occupied.

She mulled over what she'd heard. The pirates were looking for a corporate test lab. Did it have anything to do with the destruction of their planet? Why was he being so secretive? *He must still believe you're a spy.* "I'm not recording, just so you know. I told you I'm not a spy. How can I convince you?"

He turned slowly, his gaze raking her from head to toe. Her own gaze flicked downward to the obvious bulge at his crotch, and her lower region tightened in response. The sudden return of sexual tension in the room made it difficult to breathe. She licked her lips, remembering the kiss. Hot guys rarely looked twice at her, but he was definitely looking. Maybe she did know a way to convince him...

"You need to go in there," he pointed to an open door to his right, through which she could see a large bed. Tingles washed across her body and her panties heated with dampness. *Yes, please.* She turned toward the door to comply, and he continued speaking. "And as soon as we reach port, I want you off my ship."

She halted, looking over her shoulder. "Wait, what?"

He stood in the same spot, hands clenched into fists at his sides. "I can't have you around me."

Understanding dawned on her. She slowly turned to face him, her desire burning into anger. "What is it you're afraid of, Kashatok? Is it all women, or is it just me?"

His eyes sparked with repressed anger. "I am not afraid of you. I'm afraid *for* you. Do you have any idea how close you were to destruction a few moments ago?"

"No, because you won't tell me." She crossed her arms. "This could all be resolved by talking."

He bared his teeth. "You want me to tell you? All right. How's this? The denaidan mating ritual is deadly to humans."

Her mouth fell open. *Well, that was unexpected.* "Uh, mating ritual?"

"During intercourse, my species creates an empathic connection so strong, it kills non-denaidan females." His gaze was so intense she almost believed him.

Almost.

She shifted her weight to one hip. "So that explains you banning human females. But why don't you just bring denaidan women on board?"

He looked longingly at the rum bottle sitting on the desk. "Our females are all dead."

Her brows drew together. *All* dead? Gassy'd told her a bit about the destruction of his world in between the last couple of burn cycles. She still had trouble believing Syndicorp would do such a thing, but he was fairly convincing, and she'd grown to trust the old man in the short time she'd known him. Strange that he'd neglected to mention this business about mating rituals, especially since he apparently knew her secret all along. "Are you saying all your women were destroyed with your planet?"

"Our women's empathic abilities were too sensitive. They were incapable of interacting with other species. There were none off-planet."

She realized she should be recording this and engaged

her camera. "Have you ever actually reported any of this?"

He scowled. "Not personally."

"Then humor me." She took a step toward the desk. "I'll make sure the galaxy knows."

His eyes tightened, and he held up one palm. "Stop right there. How about you humor *me*, first? It took a lot of nerve to disguise yourself as a boy and board my ship after being warned about the consequences. Why do you want to film us so badly?"

She stopped. If keeping her distance got him to talk, she'd shout from the moon. Not that she felt she could stay away from him for long. He drew her like a magnet drew iron filings. "I'm a reporter. That's my job."

"No. You're a mechanic. A damned good one if you're keeping up with Gassy. A real reporter would've had her camera running this entire time. You just began recording a moment ago."

The heat infusing her face grew nearly unbearable. How did he know? "I… was trying to be polite."

He laughed. "A polite reporter. I buy that even less than your disguise."

She put her hands on her hips. "Hey! It took several days and a jump across open space for you to figure it out."

"I was drunk." He picked up the nearby bottle and rolled it between his hands. "Besides, Gassy figured it out."

"He's smarter than you are." The dig made him blanch. *Good.* He needed to learn she wouldn't put up with bullying. Jhikik tapped her pant leg with one paw and she bent to pick him up. "I've told you the truth. Lock me up if you need to."

He looked up from the bottle, one eye twitching slightly. "I just tried to, and you refused."

"You did?"

He gestured toward the bedroom.

"Oh. That. I thought you wanted me in there for another reason."

Now it was his turn to blush, an adorable bluish green. *Had she seriously just thought this fierce alien pirate was adorable?* He cleared his throat. "Now you know better."

She watched the blush fade. "That other captain you just talked to. He had a woman on board."

The softness that had come with Kashatok's blush solidified into the familiar angry lines she was used to. "Not you, too."

"Me too, what? Does this have something to do with the nanites Gassy was talking about?"

"The nanites are a false hope." Something about Kasha-tok's expression made her think he wanted that hope, even if he kept pushing it away.

Much as she wanted to smooth the furious lines from his face, she knew better than to approach him. Instead, she plucked a leaf from inside the cage and offered it to Jhikik. He nibbled it delicately, purring in her ear. "Please don't stop talking."

He exhaled slowly. "Stop recording."

She'd forgotten she was. Nodding, she stopped her camera. Her personal curiosity was stronger than her need to film.

Looking closely at her face, he seemed to decide she'd done as he asked. "That woman you saw supposedly stole some Syndicorp biotech that made her telepathic to computers or some such bullshit. As a side effect, the nanites changed her synapses enough to allow her to bond with a denaidan."

Joy broke into an involuntary grin. "That's great news! How many of you have bonded?"

"She's the only one. And she almost died during the process."

"Oh." Joy bit her lip and noticed his gaze shift to her mouth. Her stomach fluttered. "Have other women tried?"

Kashatok turned away. "Not that I'm aware of. But it's not like I'm tracking it."

"But you're wanting women to try."

"*I'm* wanting nothing." He slammed a palm against his desk, shaking the nearby bottle. "Now, can we stop talking about this?"

She gave Jhikik another leaf and ran her fingertips over the maroon petals of a flower, watching it close in response to her touch. She'd get no more out of him right now. "Thank you for telling me."

"Will you lock yourself up now?"

"No." Joy raised an eyebrow. This guy had a single solution for everything. "But I will go to engineering and wait for the other ship."

When the boarding tube connected, she planned on being front and center. She had a few questions for this Captain Qaiyaan.

Kashatok paced the room, waiting for an update from the other ship. Every few minutes he strolled down the corridor and past the open door to engineering, worried about Joy alone in there with his crew mucking about. He'd warned her to keep up her disguise as she'd left his cabin, but for all he knew, Gassy was babbling the secret to everyone in his drug-induced stupor. The old engineer had been sound asleep every time he passed the med bay.

Damn that woman. She had no idea how close she'd come to becoming a turnip with that kiss. The memory of it laced a fiery trail through his veins and settled with low, hard heat in his cock. It had been hours, yet he throbbed against his pants. If he hadn't been interrupted, he had no idea how far he might've taken things.

How long had it been since he'd even wanted a woman? Really wanted one? The few he had to interact with while in port never lingered in his mind. He glared at the bottle on his desk. Then again, he usually drowned himself in rum. He knew how to ride a fine line with the intoxicant, drinking enough to dull his desires but keep him functional for duty.

But desires were easy to dull when the object of them was far out of reach, and he made a point of never staying in port long enough to crack his reserve. With Joy right here on the ship, it was all he could do to keep himself from storming into engineering and taking her hard against the control panel. Or in the parts locker. Or on the floor… He glanced into his open bedroom and imagined her splayed out on the crisp, clean sheets.

Whirling, he grabbed the bottle and threw it, shattering it against the far wall. Even sober, he could barely keep his mind and his hands off her. He couldn't afford to have the stuff sitting around taunting him.

Closing his eyes, he sighed, remembering her slight frame pressed against his back during the jump between ships. Now he had the sensation of her limbs seared against his front as well, her soft belly pressed against his raging hard-on. The wet and willing pressure of her mouth—oh, her mouth—he wanted to devour her.

If he wasn't careful, he would.

One wrong move from him would empty her mind of all its contents forever. Much as he preferred not to, he forced himself to picture Aiyana's blank stare. Why couldn't he remember her face? When he tried to recall those dead eyes, that slack mouth, all he could see was Joy's liquid brown eyes and the delightful way she was always chewing her bottom lip. Very alive.

Jhikik, sensing his distress, chirped and clawed his pant leg. Out of habit, he picked the little creature up and set him on his shoulder. The long tail with its suction cups curled up under his arm and gripped his chest, making him think of Joy's hands against his sides. What if the nanites worked? Could they possibly make her strong enough to withstand the passion of a killer like him?

No. The idea was nonsense, and thinking about it would only invite trouble. As soon as Captain Qaiyaan arrived, Kashatok would transfer her. Get her out of danger. She was a talented mechanic. Maybe Qaiyaan would swap his engineer for her.

As soon as Kashatok came up with the idea, he rejected it. No way he'd put her in Qaiyaan's hands with the nanites right there. What if the bastard slipped them to her? The man was obviously dead set on making mates. Those damned Syndicorp machines could fry her brain as easily as Kashatok would if he took her on the floor in engineering.

The comm pinged. Kashatok stalked to his desk, his mind in a fury.

A bearded face appeared on-screen. "Captain Kashatok, we're approaching the asteroid belt."

Holding back a string of unwarranted curse words, Kashatok replied, "Acknowledged, Captain. I'll turn on our locator."

Qaiyaan ran his fingers down the twin braids under his chin. "Have you discovered any information about that lab?"

Uminaq. The lab. Back when Captain Qaiyaan first contacted him with the request, Kashatok'd done a quick overview of his informant's notes, mostly out of personal curiosity. But he hadn't bothered to actually offer to pay the cartel to dig up the information not already out there on the darkweb. That kind of intel was expensive, and Qaiyaan wasn't a wealthy captain. Even his bucket-of-bolts ship was worth less than Kashatok's usual payout.

Now the *Hardship* was going to pull his ass out of the fire. He guessed he owed him. "My initial assessment doesn't show excessive trooper activity in any of the systems that might indicate they're guarding a secret lab. I do recall a couple that have a suspicious *lack* of Syndicorp traffic. Sometimes that's as good an indicator as excess vessel movement. I'll ask my informants as soon as I reach a port."

Qaiyaan's eyes narrowed. "Is this the first you've looked into it? You know how important this information could be. Not just to me. To all of us. We need a renewable source of nanites."

Kashatok cleared his throat. "Yeah. Have you infected any other women yet?"

A muscle in Qaiyaan's jaw bulged. "No. And it's not an infection."

"My mistake." Kashatok didn't hide the sarcasm in his tone. As he'd suspected, the nanites were a hoax. Still, if information was what the guy wanted, it was a fair price for a ride out of here. "I'll contact you when I have information."

"That's what you said last time." Qaiyaan's holographic face grew larger as he leaned forward. "How about you send out that request right now? I'll wait."

Sighing, Kashatok shook his head. None of the so-called pirates in the fleet really understood what it meant to be a criminal. "I never put cartel requests out via comm or the darkweb. Not even on secure channels."

"Awful convenient excuse. Maybe I should leave you here to think about it while I go track down your part. How much juice do you have left for life support?"

Kashatok grit his teeth. He had to admit, he'd basically ignored Qaiyaan's previous request. He wasn't exactly a pay-it-forward kind of guy, and he'd owed the captain nothing. "Listen, that intel's going to be expensive. I couldn't front the money when you asked before. This time I owe you, so I'll make sure I follow up. The sooner you get us out of here, the sooner I can work on it. If there's a Syndicorp lab around here, you'll know in a few days."

Qaiyaan cast him a disgusted look over the holo, gave a curt nod, and cut the transmission.

Kashatok stood staring at the empty space above his desk for a moment, then he hit the comm and told the bridge to engage the ship's locater. He prayed Qaiyaan didn't make him wait out of spite.

Chapter Eight

Joy'd been mulling over her options for hours while she puttered in the cargo bay waiting for the other ship. Kashatok's sudden and urgent kiss had left her breathless. Never had a guy as hot as this broody alien pirate even batted an eye in her direction. He made her feel stupid and giddy, like she was thirteen again with dreams of movie star boyfriends.

Don't get involved. He'd just kissed her because she was the only woman around. She wasn't glamorous. Even Mother called her plain. Her few sexual encounters had been nothing worth mentioning, and she had no spectacular skills in that department. Give Kashatok a selection of other women and she'd surely be the last pick.

Besides, on board this ship, she was a reporter, and she needed to think like one. How many filming opportunities had she missed already? No more. If she had to keep her camera rolling until the resulting headache knocked her out, she would. Her gritty pirate exposé had shifted, becoming the heartbreaking story of a species' hopeless cause, of cover-ups and revenge, of stolen technology and sex. It was going to blow her ratings off the charts. As for the nanites, well, if the chance came along, she'd take it. The mechanic in her was intrigued by the little robots. She'd thought her camera was the coolest thing ever when it was installed. What would it be like to have tiny computers at her beck and call?

The comm lit up with a call from the bridge. "All hands, prepare to be boarded."

Excitement surged in her chest. She wiped her hands on a nearby grease rag and engaged her camera. Two pirate ships meeting had to be something special, and she wanted to be sure to capture every interaction. Hurrying to the cargo bay, she joined the rest of the crew. As she panned their faces, she realized that although they seemed relaxed, every one of them was armed.

Kashatok strode between them without a glance in her direction and proceeded to the bay door just as it hissed open. Her ears popped at the sudden change in pressure.

A tall, shaggy-haired man she recognized as Captain Qaiyaan stood on the boarding tube's other side, just as broadly imposing as all the other denaidans. "Permission to come aboard, Captain?"

Her captain was armed, as well, she noted. "Granted."

Qaiyaan crossed over, followed by a younger denaidan with hair as copper as his skin.

Joy focused in on the younger man's bare feet, curious, panning upward to meet his gaze. He grinned at her, and she couldn't stop herself from grinning back.

Captain Qaiyaan asked, "Who's your engineer?"

Kashatok shook his head. "Gassy was injured." He gestured Joy's direction without looking at her. "The kid and I've taken the repairs as far as we can."

The younger copper-skinned man strode right over and stuck out his hand. "Hi, I'm Tovik. You're an engineer? *Assirpaa!*"

She didn't know what *assirpaa* meant, but he seemed genuinely excited. "Mechanic, actually," she said, holding out a hand. "Name's Joey."

"Nice to meet you, Joy. I thought Kashatok didn't allow women on his ship!"

Joy froze, her attention sliding to Kashatok. The entire cargo bay went silent, and the crew seemed to turn toward her in slow motion. She felt like a mouse in a den of cats. Apparently oblivious, Tovik kept grinning, and she realized she still held his hand. She dropped it and backed up a step, scrambling for a comeback. "You trying to insult me?"

But it was too late. Cooper and Moore had their heads together, muttering. Manopup's tentacles writhed like snakes around his chin. Aleknagik stared at her with predatory eyes. Chignik laughed and slapped Ekwok on the back. "I thought there was something off about the kid."

Kashatok closed in, forcing Tovik to take a step back. "How did you know?"

The poor young man's mouth hung open. He looked over his shoulder at his captain. "Isn't it obvious?"

Qaiyaan took a step forward. "Come here, Tovik."

Tovik slumped back toward his captain. "I knew I should've just stayed in engineering. I'm never going to find a mate."

All around her, the crew continued murmuring. The word "nanites" surfaced several times, along with "sex" and several more obscene references.

"So who does she belong to?" Qaiyaan asked, looking around at the denaidans.

Joy stiffened. "Belong to? I belong to myself."

Qaiyaan looked from her to Kashatok and back to her as if verifying she was telling the truth. Then he dipped his head toward her. "My apologies, Joy. Knowing Kashatok, I assumed…"

"You assumed wrong," Kashatok said.

Joy's stomach churned. Knowing Kashatok? What did that mean? She looked at her captain, but he kept his focus on Qaiyaan, his fists like hammers at his sides. She'd have to grill him for answers on that later. For now, she stepped in between the two captains. "It's a long story, Captain Qaiyaan. But I'm the closest thing the Kinship has to an engineer right now." Reminding the crew of how important she was couldn't hurt. "How about I escort Tovik to our engine room and start working on getting us out of here?"

"I believe Tovik needs you to go with him first." Qaiyaan stepped to the side and held a hand out in invitation. "To go over our ship's burn schematics so you can match up during piggyback. I'd hate to get the alignment wrong and fling you into another galaxy."

"If you send the schematics over, we can review them here," Joy said.

Qaiyaan shook his head. "We won't release specific details about our ship." His gaze cut toward Kashatok. "Especially not to a cartel informant."

Gassy'd mentioned Kashatok was the only cartel member in the fleet, but Joy hadn't realized there was animosity about it. Shrugging, she took a step forward.

Kashatok's hand on her arm halted her. "I'm coming, too."

Qaiyaan thrust out one hand, his other close by his pulse pistol. "I'd prefer you stayed aboard your own vessel, captain."

Kashatok's grip on her arm grew firmer. "I'm not comfortable letting her go alone."

Joy gently pried his fingers loose. "I'll be fine, captain."

He dropped his hand, but she could see by the heaving of his chest he didn't agree. Spearing her with a dark look, he said, "I need to speak to you. Now."

"Of course." Acting more self-assured than she felt, she followed him to the far corner of the cargo bay. Ekwok bobbed his tawny head thoughtfully as she passed by, his eyebrows high. She refused to notice anyone else, but she could feel their attention like lasers following her movement.

Rounding the nose of the shuttle, Kashatok turned and gripped both her biceps. "I don't trust him not to take off with you once you're on board. Without functional drives, I can't follow you."

At the physical contact, her nipples had hardened involuntarily, yearning for his thumbs to spread inward and tease them. How did this man banish all sense of reason within her? Perhaps his caveman-like attitude was pushing her biological buttons. Whatever it was, she liked it, but now wasn't the time for such things. "Why would he take off with me?"

"He has the nanites."

She waited for more explanation, but he apparently believed he'd said enough. Shrugging free of his grip, she tried to give him a reassuring smile. "Kashatok, there is no reason he would steal me away. There are countless numbers of women throughout the galaxy he can give nanites to."

"The nanites are stolen Syndicorp tech. He can't just give them to anyone."

"If that's true, he won't force them on me. Stop trying to hide me away."

His jaw muscles bulged as he ground his teeth and his chest still heaved, but he obviously couldn't argue. "I don't like it."

A warm feeling welled up inside her. She'd never felt protected by someone before, had never thought she'd like it, especially since her mother was so overbearing. But Kashatok's emotion was so raw and genuine, it wasn't about control for the sake of control. He was truly worried about her.

She checked over her shoulder to be sure no one could see, then playfully tugged the end of his beard. It was too bad he'd left Jhikik back in his cabin; the little netorpok might've given him comfort. "I know you just want to keep me safe, but Captain Qaiyaan came all the way here to help us before he even knew I was aboard. I don't think he'll harm me."

"What if he doesn't let you come back?"

"Why would he do that?"

"The other pirate captains don't trust me."

Joy tilted her head. "But he came to help you."

Kashatok rubbed his forehead, his face tight. "Denaidans help other denaidans. There're too few of us left not to. But they don't trust me with women, and for good reason."

She made a show of turning off her camera. This was something personal, and she wanted him to feel free to talk. "Tell me why. Please."

Tiny muscles twitched on his cheeks as if it took everything he had to keep himself in check. "It's complicated. Now's not the time or place."

She leaned closer, making sure she had full eye contact. "When I get back?"

He closed his eyes, letting out a shallow breath before nodding sharply.

"All right. I have an idea." She leaned around the shuttle to look at Qaiyaan. Aleknagik had moved forward and was talking to the other captain. Tovik laughed at something they said, and the rest of the crew joined in. She turned back to Kashatok. "Ask him to leave one of his other crewmen behind as collateral. He won't abandon his own man."

Kashatok inhaled slowly and released it. "You're suggesting a hostage, of sorts."

He didn't move for a long moment, just looking at her, and her heart threatened to beat out of her chest. It felt like he might want another kiss. He smelled so good, like nutmeg and smoke. She licked her lips.

Gazing at her mouth, he reached out and brushed her lips with one thumb. "Don't let them talk you into anything stupid. All right?"

She nodded, every nerve ending alight with his nearness.

Then he pulled away and stalked toward the gathered crew.

Regaining her presence of mind took a moment. When her legs felt steady, she hurried to catch up, trying hard not to stare at his amazing backside. The irony wasn't lost on her; she was ogling him while the crew was obviously thinking similar things about her. Sweat prickled her skin under the crew's watchful eyes, but she kept her head high.

Kashatok stopped several feet from the other captain. "She'll go with you, but we need one of your crewmen to stay here while she's gone."

Moving into place at Kashatok's side, she caught Tovik's eye and winked. The stiffness in the young man's shoulders eased, and he winked back. This could all be worked out if she could just keep them talking.

"Agreed." Qaiyaan tapped a spot below his ear. "Noatak, you're needed on the *Kinship*."

Kashatok added, "And don't mess with her head. She's my only engineer."

The warmth she'd felt earlier cooled a little. Engineer. Right. That's why he needed her safe. She'd been reading way too much into the kiss.

Noatak arrived—a big denaidan with thick black hair kept in check with wide silver bands along its length—and after a moment of hushed discussion between him and Qaiyaan, Joy followed Tovik aboard the *Hardship*.

A hard lump blocked her throat as she crossed the boarding tube. She entered the much smaller cargo bay of the *Hardship* close on Tovik's heels, expecting him to continue toward the stairs leading to a grated catwalk ahead. Only a few steps inside, he spun, stopping her short. "Orders, Captain?"

Qaiyaan cycled the atmosphere shield up behind them, hazing out the view into the *Kinship's* bay. Joy's stomach clenched, and not only because the gravity on this side was lower than she was used to. Kashatok might've been right. "What's going on? I thought we were going to look at schematics."

A charcoal-haired woman bounded down the catwalk stairs, spotted Joy, and slowed. Joy felt a strange desire to cringe. To turn tail and run back down the boarding tube.

The woman was even more stunning in person than she'd been on the holo-screen, wearing a form-fitting tank top and black leather pants, rounded in all the right places. Her perfect, heart-shaped face and creamy skin made Joy feel absolutely swarthy. Joy brushed both palms ineffectually down the front of her shirt and onto her thighs, as if that might magically change her grease-stained work clothes into a pirelux suit.

The captain held an arm out and the other woman ducked under it, wrapping her arm around his waist. He said, "Joy, meet Lisa, my mate."

"A woman?" Awareness dawned on Lisa's face and she scrolled her gaze down Joy's body. "I thought you said this Kashatok fellow didn't allow females on his ship?"

Joy glared at the woman. She'd met this type plenty of times; sexy, confident, and dismissive of those they considered beneath them. Her mother was that way. Joy stood taller, looking down at the shorter female and lacing her words with sarcasm. "A pleasure to meet you, too."

The woman's pale skin flushed pink, and she lowered her gaze. "I'm sorry. I didn't mean to be rude. It's just that I didn't expect you." She raised her eyes to meet Joy's. "Can we start again? I'm Lisa."

Joy nodded politely. She didn't trust this woman any more than she currently trusted these men. "Why did you bring me over here?"

A clean-shaven denaidan appeared at the top of the stairs and leaped down what had to be fifteen steps in a single bound. His eyes widened as he approached. "A woman?"

Lisa elbowed him. "Be polite."

What was it with this crew and their rude introductions? Joy thrust out a hand. "I'm Joy. Interim engineer for the *Kinship*."

"Mekoryuk, but you can call me Mek." He took her hand, a smile toying with his lips. "I'm delighted to have you aboard."

"Now that the introductions are over, I need to get back to the *Kinship* and finish repairs."

"Take a breath," Qaiyaan said. "You're safe now, and welcome to stay. Kashatok can't hurt you here."

"Kashatok would never hurt me." Joy realized as she said it how much her opinion had evolved in only a couple of days.

The three men exchanged a glance.

"What?" Joy asked.

"Kashatok has a reputation," Qaiyaan said.

"He leaves dead women at every port!" Tovik's green eyes went wide.

Joy's hand fluttered to her throat. His words a short while earlier floated through her mind; *they don't trust me with women, and for good reason.*

"Not dead, Tovik," Mek said. "Comatose."

Comatose—were they saying Kashatok was trying to mate with women in every port?

"Same thing." Tovik scowled. "They ain't getting up again, are they?"

Not Kashatok. She didn't believe he was capable of such a thing, not with how he kept pushing her away. Not with how he wanted to protect her. Joy found her voice. "You must be mistaken. Kashatok would never do that."

"You know about our mating effects?" Mek tilted his head as if reassessing her.

She nodded firmly. "Kashatok told me all about how you can't be with women and how the nanites are supposed to fix that."

Qaiyaan crossed his arms. "Asked you to get them, did he? Probably wants a toy with a longer battery life."

Joy gritted her teeth. "I'm not a toy. And no, he didn't ask me."

The captain's cocky attitude turned to confusion. "He didn't?"

"He told me to stay away. Wants me off his ship as soon as possible. If he didn't fear you'd infect me with nanites against my will, he'd ask you to take me off his hands for good."

Mek held both palms out. "Let's be clear here: the nanites are not an infection."

"And we'd never do anything against your will!" Tovik insisted.

All the men started talking at once until Lisa put her fingers in her mouth and emitted a sharp whistle. Joy's assessment of her improved another notch. "All of you, be quiet."

The men grumbled but quieted.

Lisa put her hands on her hips. "What's important here is what Joy wants." Lisa turned to look Joy in the eye. "So let her speak."

Joy's throat went suddenly dry. What did she want? These pirates had stumbled upon top-secret Syndicorp tech that could allow them to hack into galactic banks or steal military secrets, and yet all they wanted to do with it was to create mates. If she was honest with herself, she no longer cared about the exposé. She hadn't even turned her camera back on after talking to Kashatok. She honestly wanted to fix the *Kinship* and make Kashatok value her enough to keep her aboard. And maybe, just maybe, explore this mating ritual thing.

But to do that, she'd need the nanites.

Her pulse thundered in her ears as she said, "I'd like to know a little more about those nanites, please."

CHAPTER NINE

Kashatok paced the big bay, pretending to catalog non-existent cargo while he waited for Joy to return. At the back of the cavernous space, his crew sat around a cargo-container-turned-card-table playing the slowest game of Ongaru Flip Kashatok'd ever seen.

The *Hardship's* first mate had fit in among the men as easily as if he was one of them rather than what amounted to a hostage. The thick bands of silver in his long hair made him stand out among the slightly rougher crew, who seemed to hang on his every word while he spoke animatedly about the nanites. "It took me awhile to believe it, too, and I was right there. But believe me, if you could hear the noise coming from the captain's quarters every night, you'd believe it's possible, too."

Chignik tilted his head back and groaned. *"Ellam Cua,* to experience a woman again."

Nodding in agreement, Ekwok leaned forward. "Noatak, please, will you give the nanites to our female?"

Kashatok bristled at the term "our." This was just what he'd feared; the crew wanted her. Were already plotting to have her. *She's mine.* The thought rose up inside him in a primal wave, and he clenched his fists at his sides, trying to squash it down. He was no better than they were if he thought like that. He needed to keep himself and his crew in check. Perhaps he should ask Captain Qaiyaan to keep her on board the *Hardship* and avoid the whole thing. But once again, that primal possessiveness rose inside him. *Mine.*

Noatak continued, "The choice is up to her. I doubt she'd want them if she's not attached to a denaidan."

Jhikik appeared out of nowhere, digging his claws into Kashatok's pant leg and scurrying to his shoulder. The little *tunrak* must've escaped through the vents again, but for once, Kashatok was glad. He needed the little guy's calming effect. He stroked the soft tail as it hugged his neck. "Don't worry, Jhik. She'll be back."

Jhikik made a high-pitched noise and settled into a crouch.

At the game table, Cooper slapped a card on the center pile, waving away the bottle being passed around. "I'm glad I don't have to rely on some damned microcomputers to get lucky. Wonder if the captain will let her stay on board a while?"

Moore snorted and shuffled his hand. "I'll wait for the next brothel, thank you. I prefer my bed partners to look like women."

A few of the men laughed. Chignik shook his head. "She's not that bad."

"You have obviously not been around women much," Manopup said, his tentacles waggling suggestively.

"One more thing," Noatak said, playing his turn. "Not every woman's brain structure will be suitable. The nanites could be deadly."

Aleknagik finished a long swig of rum and thrust the bottle at Moore. "I don't care a damn about her brain structure, as long as her girly parts are in the right place."

Without thinking, Kashatok all but leaped across the bay to the table, looming over the players. The chatter cut off. "There will be no more talk of Joy's girly parts, and she's not going to take the nanites, so get her out of your mind."

The astonished faces broke eye contact with him one by one. All but Aleknagik. "Interesting that you gave her the option for a solo bunk room, captain."

Kashatok's dual hearts slammed hard against his ribcage while his crew exchanged questioning and suspicious glances. *Hadn't Aleknagik offered her that deal?* Kashatok honestly couldn't remember. He took a menacing step toward his first mate. "Just what are you suggesting?"

"Difficult to respect a captain who breaks his own rules."

"Hey, now, hey!" Noatak rose from his seat, making calming motions with his hands.

Just then, a hiss indicated the boarding tube shield had dilated.

Joy stepped into the bay.

Joy's mind buzzed with nanite activity. That was the only way to describe the sensation in her head. They were having a party along her optic nerve, right where her camera interfaced with her cerebral cortex. After she'd learned more about the nanites, the mechanic in her was even more fascinated. The things were supposed to allow her to hack into computer systems, of all things. Imagine how easy diagnostics could be with that kind of tech in her head? Not only that, she wanted to see if that kiss Kashatok had given her meant anything. If it hadn't, she'd at least be helping these men increase their supply of nanites and doing something to make up for the damage Syndicorp had done to these people. Not that they could ever know she was in any way affiliated with the corp'. That was one secret she needed to keep fully and completely.

Because of her cybernetic implant, Mek had been able to streamline the synaptic insertion. He'd wanted to keep her aboard the *Hardship* for observation, since she'd just received one of the two remaining nanite samples in their possession. But Joy knew Kashatok was probably blowing a gasket by now, so she'd made a deal to bring Tovik along so he could monitor her.

She stepped off the boarding tube and into the *Kinship,* leaving Tovik to maneuver the hover container carrying specialty parts across the walkway. The moment she emerged, Jhikik came bounding across the deck and leaped into her arms. "Hey, little guy. I missed you, too."

Looking up, she met Kashatok's concerned gaze across the wide bay. Behind him, his men had risen from their seats around a cargo container. Several game cards fluttered to the floor.

In a burst of motion, Kashatok strode over, his face once more bearing his usual scowl. "Well?"

She'd meant to tell him she'd taken the nanites, but hadn't pictured an audience. Instead, she gestured behind her, where Tovik was emerging from the boarding tube. "Tovik wants to install a burn harness, but I'm nervous about trying without Gassy's help." More than nervous, actually. A ship that got caught in another ship's burn wake could be flung to an unknown location, even another galaxy—and not always in one piece. The harness would create an invisible field that aligned each ship's frequency and, in effect, turn the two ships into a single unit, at least for purposes of the burn. "I'm not an engineer. What if I mess something up?"

Tovik stopped beside her, his bare feet and easy smile out of place among the crew. But the kid seemed to have eyes only for her. "Aw, you got this, Joy. I'm here every step of the way."

"I appreciate that." She smiled back gently. Tovik was obviously in puppy-love, and just as obviously had little experience with women. She wanted to tread carefully around him.

Kashatok wasn't as gentle. "She and I can handle it. Dismissed."

Tovik's face fell. "But you need to pilot the ship."

"Aleknagik can handle it."

"Damn straight," his first mate agreed.

Tovik's eyes darted nervously between the two men. "I'm also supposed to stick close to her in case the nanites go haywire."

As if with one breath, the surrounding crew seemed to gasp. "She took 'em."

"I thought they were dangerous?"

"What happens now?"

Joy's gut clenched, and she bit down hard on her lower lip. This was not how she'd wanted Kashatok to find out. And it'd definitely not been her intention to tell the entire crew.

Kashatok met her gaze, his eyes roiling with a maelstrom of horror, anger, and... hope? "I told you the nanites were dangerous. Why would you take them?"

Joy nibbled her lip, stopping self-consciously as his eyes followed the movement. "I already had a cybernetic implant, so my brain's used to interfacing. Mek says he thinks it'll be easy for me."

The Hardship's doctor had also pointed out that since she'd be surrounded by denaidans, the nanites would protect her if someone got "a little rowdy," as he put it.

He'd also given her a small pulse pistol, which she now wore at her belt.

Kashatok let out a string of curses in that guttural language the denaidans spoke. She thought she heard both Qaiyaan's and Mek's names squished in there.

Chignik moved toward her almost reverently, causing Jhikik to scurry from her arms and perch on her shoulder. The netorpok bared his blunt teeth and Chignik halted, his gaze never leaving Joy's face. "How do you feel?"

Tuliak, usually so quiet he was forgotten, murmured, "Hopefully horny."

The burst of laughter from the crew cut off as Kashatok rounded on the group behind him. "Anyone who touches Joy without her permission will get worse than space-locked."

Tovik's eyes were nearly bugging from his head. "What could be worse than space-locking?"

Leaning close, Kashatok nearly breathed fire with his next words. "You don't want to find out."

Joy made a cutting motion between Kashatok and the young engineer. The tension was making the slight headache from the nanites worse. "No one's touching me and no one's getting space-locked. We have much bigger issues at hand." She grabbed the handhold at one corner of the hover container. "Qaiyaan detected a trooper ship back in the area, so we need to get this thing installed and burn out of here before they find us."

Kashatok's snarl relaxed enough to be called a scowl once again. "*Uminaq.* Fine. You two get to work. I'm going to have a word with Qaiyaan." He bored into Tovik with a gaze that could cut through hull plating. "I'll be back soon."

To his credit, Tovik stood his ground.

The denaidan who'd stayed aboard the *Kinship* stepped forward. "I'll escort you over." The big man slowed as he passed Joy, his gaze curious. "Got to say, you're one ballsy woman, coming back here. I'd keep a blaster close if I were you."

Joy didn't answer him. She wasn't sure if she was ballsy or just plain stupid.

Kashatok focused on Joy before he headed toward the docking tube. "You're my mechanic. Remember that. Do not put up with any *anaq* from the others."

This time, the way he called her "my mechanic" filled her with a new flutter of hope. His words felt possessive. Personal. A lightness seemed to blossom right below her heart, filling her stomach with butterflies. Unable to help herself, she beamed at him and pulled the hover container between the surrounding crew toward engineering.

Entering the familiar space, she paused. The room seemed full of motion, even though there were no moving parts within view. Was it the nanites increasing her awareness? Lisa had told her she might begin to sense computer systems as the nanites populated her synapses, but she shouldn't expect any immediate changes. Like her camera implant, it would take time to train her brain to use the nanites once they began working. She tried to focus on the console across the room but received nothing out of the ordinary, so she moved toward the workbench and helped Tovik unload the elaborate contraption of metal and flux tubing he called a harness. He stroked a palm over the part's shiny metal face. "We'll need to splice this into your main burn drive. Is the power supply off?"

She turned to the nearby console. Without even calling up the information, she knew the circuit to the burn drive was disconnected. Excited, she swept her gaze over the controls and received a reading from the gravity generator telling her all systems were within acceptable parameters. *Wow.* These nanites were going to be useful.

Still unsure it was all real, she tapped the controls and manually reassured herself that the system powering the burn drive was off. "Ready."

Together, they manipulated the harness between the mess of pipes in the jungle. Halfway through securing the harness, she had a new understanding of why Gassy called it a jungle. Both she and Tovik had to invent new ways to bend and twist to access the connections, while Jhikik clambered among the conduits overhead, seemingly unwilling to let her out of his sight. Currently, she lay on her back on the floor beneath a large duct, stretching one arm overhead toward one cable while holding two other cables near her belly button to keep them from escaping. She couldn't quite reach her target. "Damn it, I could use a third arm in here."

On his hands and knees, Tovik squeezed his wide shoulders into the small space next to her. "You sure you're on the right set of circuits?"

With a sudden yelp, he toppled forward. Just as abruptly, he was yanked backward out of the hole.

"What the hell do you think you're doing?" Kashatok's low voice rattled the metal duct above her face.

"*Anaq*, dude!" The sound of scuffling reached her. "We're just modulating the shield phasing. You want us to crack each other like eggs on our first piggyback?"

Letting go of her cables, Joy wriggled herself free. Kashatok's fists held Tovik's tunic and the black expression on his face would be enough to make a rakwiji male go limp.

"Kashatok, it's okay." She moved forward to stop him.

The captain gave Tovik a hard shove, sending him stumbling backward against the nearby console. The panel lit up at the impact, and a wave of data hurtled outward. It slammed into Joy's mind like a pulse blast. Out of habit from over a year practicing with her camera, she threw up her data override protocols. But the incoming wave was huge.

Her vision went dark. Tovik's angry response to Kashatok was lost to her as she stumbled backward, blinking.

Blinking.

Blinking.

She pressed both palms against her eye sockets and released them while information twittered incomprehensibly through her consciousness. Her veins slowly turned to ice. She felt like she could no longer breathe under the onslaught. Just before her legs collapsed beneath her, she gasped, "Kashatok, I can't see."

Chapter Ten

Kashatok hovered over Mek's shoulder, watching the doctor run a scanner over Joy's head for at least the fifth time. She lay unconscious on the cot in the *Hardship's* medical bay while Jhikik, refusing to stray more than an arm's length away from her shoulder, clicked a warning every time the doctor's hand moved closer to her. Kashatok knew how he felt.

The instant Joy'd collapsed, he'd scooped her up and rushed to the *Hardship's* medical bay. Qaiyaan and Lisa had met him at the boarding tube and now the couple stood close together at the far corner of the medical bay, murmuring softly together. The part of him that wasn't intent on the dire situation envied the way they seemed to act as extensions of each other.

Mek set the scanner aside and turned to face Kashatok and the others. "I can't yet determine if the damage to her optic nerve is permanent."

Kashatok needed to punch someone. Or he needed a drink. "Why didn't you warn her this could happen?"

Mek stared at his scanner. "I warned her there would be side effects, but we didn't count on the nanites populating her synapses this fast. She's nearly fully integrated already."

Lisa sighed, her face flushed pink. "I should've remembered. At the Syndicorp lab, people with existing cybernetics stabilized at least ten times faster than people like me. My brother was using the nanites to hack the lab's computer the very next day."

Kashatok examined the soft curve of Joy's face. *Ellam Cua.* He wanted to touch her, to physically make sure she was still breathing. His gaze slid to her chest where her breasts were barely noticeable mounds beneath her tunic. She wasn't pinup-girl curvy, but she was definitely female. How could he have ever thought otherwise? Dragging his attention away from her breasts, he shoved his hands in his pockets and satisfied himself with the reassuring beat of her heart through his ionic senses. "When will she wake up?"

"I'm not sure," Mek said. "Her brain waves indicate she's cognizant of what's going on and it appears the nanites are working in tandem with her cybernetic implant. I'm hoping that's a good thing. But awake or not, she's going to need to stay on the *Hardship* for observation."

Of course. They'd probably planned this all along. Well, he wasn't leaving her. Kashatok settled back on a nearby stool. "Just tell me what I need to do."

"Go back to the *Kinship* and get ready for piggyback," Qaiyaan said. "Those troopers are scanning the asteroid field only a few kilometers away."

"My first mate can handle the *Kinship*." Kashatok crossed his arms. "I'm staying here."

Mek and Qaiyaan exchanged a glance.

Anticipating an argument, Kashatok found himself off balance when, instead, Lisa gently took Qaiyaan's hand. "He's worried. Let him stay." She tugged her mate toward the door. "We need to bring a nav-grav buffer in here, anyway."

The two left the room and Kashatok stared morosely at Joy. The woman must have a death wish with the choices she made. He shouldn't care, should leave her here to deal with her own consequences. Hell, he should've locked her in her room when he'd first learned her secret. But he'd let her convince him she was needed. He'd been a fool.

Mek took more blood samples, filing them away in a stasis locker. For a small ship, the *Hardship's* med bay was remarkably well equipped. Jhikik continued to click, tail twitching as if ready to slap the doctor's hands away.

Unsure of what to do with himself, Kashatok asked, "What are her options now?"

Mek placed a second set of samples in a centrifuge. "The nanites act like seed cells. Over time, they make synaptic changes that will provide resistance to denaidan mating frequencies. But if allowed to progress too far, the nanites take over completely. I'm monitoring her levels. Short of terminating the nanites early, we have to wait and see."

Terminate the nanites? Kashatok bolted upright. "You mean the nanites aren't permanent? If you can get rid of them, do it now!"

Mek leveled a serious gaze at him. "There is only one way to get rid of the nanites, Captain. The denaidan mating frequency."

A lump rose in Kashatok's throat. To be rid of the nanites, Joy would have to have sex. Glorious, fulfilling, mind-boggling sex. An act Kashatok could never take part in. "You've got to be kidding. Was Joy aware of this?"

"I told her. She was remarkably unconcerned."

"*Uminaq*! Who did she..." Kashatok scrubbed his palms over his cheeks, the heated memory of kissing her washing over him. Had she envisioned him as part of the process? *Ellam Cua,* he should have made it clear that he absolutely wasn't an option. "She can't. She's unconscious."

Rubbing his nose and mouth as if reluctant to say his next words, Mek said, "She... doesn't need to be conscious."

Kashatok took a menacing step toward the doctor. "No one is touching her without her permission."

Mek stood straighter and narrowed his eyes. "You'd rather she died?"

"Of course not. But..." Kashatok scrambled for solutions. "We could engineer a frequency pulse simulation."

"Hm." Mek drummed his fingers against his chin. "We never considered we might need such an option. Truthfully, Tovik may be able to, given enough time." The doctor shook his head. "But he has his hands full overseeing the piggyback."

Kashatok wanted to volunteer. But he didn't know enough about engineering, and Gassy was out of commission. If Joy was awake, they could probably figure something out together.

"She's your crewman, so the choice is yours," Mek said. "She made it very clear that she trusts you. Maybe even more than trusts."

Kashatok didn't realize he was backing up until the stool hit the back of his legs. "Even if she was awake and asked me to, I couldn't. Can't." His heartbeats warred with each other inside his chest. In a rush, he blurted, "I'm a *carayak*!"

The word hung in the air like a toxic cloud. One, two, three heartbeats.

Mek's attention drifted toward Kashatok's groin, and Kashatok knew what he was thinking. *Why isn't he castrated?*

A small voice punched through the tension. "What's a *carayak*?"

Kashatok about jumped out of his skin. "You're awake!"

Joy's eyes remained slit, as if she was having trouble in the bright light, while Mek waved a scanner above her head. "Still no sight?"

She shook her head. "Nothing. Tell me what a *carayak* is."

"A denaidan male with an extraordinarily rare genetic condition which causes incompatible mating frequencies." Mek jerked his hand back, barely in time to avoid Jhikik's teeth.

"Deadly frequencies." The words felt like lava crawling up Kashatok's throat. "Even to other denaidans."

"Deadly?" she whispered, raising one hand to her lips. Lips he remembered kissing all too well. "But you kissed me."

"The harmful frequency is created during climax," Mek said, his voice annoyingly clinical. "It doesn't kill the female, just destroys her consciousness. Most *carayaks* discover the condition during puberty, unfortunately during their first sexual encounter." He turned to Kashatok. "I've never heard of an un-castrated adult *carayak* outside of a monastery. Have you been tested?"

Kashatok half grunted, half laughed. "Only the old-fashioned way."

The truth was out now, and no amount of rum could ever hide it again. He numbly stared into Joy's blind face, hating her unfocused eyes; they reminded him of Aiyana. But he was also glad Joy couldn't see him. He wanted her as far away from this horrible side of himself as she could get.

"That's why you don't want women on your ship," she said softly.

Mek leaned back against the counter and crossed one leg over the other, but the leisurely motion somehow only exacerbated the tension. "Captain, I have to ask. Are the rumors about you true?"

Dredging up these memories had created a hollow pit inside Kashatok's gut, like the sudden emptying of a pond that left nothing but stinking, rotting sludge behind. He may as well purge himself of all of it. "Yes. I was sixteen and her name was Aiyana." He refused to look at Joy, the hopelessness in his chest a raw wound. "And for the record, I loved her."

"And the others?" Mek asked.

"Others?" Kashatok frowned.

"The comatose women you leave in every port."

Kashatok straightened. He knew people considered him a monster, but he'd never heard that rumor. "I would never! I don't even allow women on my ship."

"Then how did you end up with her?" Mek nodded toward Joy.

Kashatok recalled the first moment he'd seen Joy, a wide-eyed, olive-skinned face in a cantina. How spunky she'd been arguing for her cut of the profits. Even though he'd thought she was a boy, something about her had drawn him.

"My fault." Joy raised her hand as if asking permission to speak in class. "I disguised myself as a man."

"I didn't find out until we were well underway," Kashatok added. "Or I would've dropped her off at the next port."

Mek scratched his cheek, his nails loud against the stubble, tilting his head to regard Kashatok. "And what about now?"

Kashatok swallowed. *What about now?* He liked having Joy around. Yet having her near could only end badly. Hell, it already had. She was fucking blind. And nanites or not, she couldn't remain on his ship. "A blind mechanic's useless to me."

From the bed, Joy sucked in a breath and turned her face away. Kashatok wanted to pound his own skull against a bulkhead. Why'd he say such a thing?

Jhikik chirped and stroked Joy's cheek with the furry side of his tail.

"I see." Mek straightened. "Well, you won't need to worry about her from here on out. She's welcome to stay on board the *Hardship*. I know Tovik won't mind."

The little voice inside Kashatok's head was chanting *mine* over and over. Another voice repeated he could never have her. Then a thought occurred to him. "Wait. Are you suggesting all she's good for now is mating?"

Mek shrugged. "Mated or not, we'll take good care of her, even if she's blind. But she'll eventually need to get rid of the nanites with someone."

Kashatok realized he'd moved to the bed as if to shield her. His ionic sense could feel her trembling, hitching, fighting tears. Tears he'd caused, and he hated himself all the more for it. "She's good at engineering. Maybe I can be her eyes and help her come up with an alternate plan to zap the nanites."

The doctor raised his brows. "As long as she allows me to draw a small supply of the nanites to inoculate future mates, we're completely open to any alternatives." Mek tapped a finger against his chin. "You know, *carayaks* are extremely rare. If you are one, you might help us understand how our mating frequencies interact with other species. Will you allow me to take a tissue sample?"

Balls tightening as he thought of the tissue Mek wanted, Kashatok considered agreeing; castration would make him safe for Joy to be around. Then he imagined the overweight, soft-voiced monks from his childhood. *No fucking way.* He turned so his shoulder faced the doctor, keeping his groin well out of reach. "I happen to like my balls right where they are."

"Not your genitals." Mek pulled a swab from the cabinet and held it up. "I just want a few tissue cells from your mouth."

Kashatok regarded the harmless swab. After a moment, he shrugged. "Fine."

Mek had just finished swabbing Kashatok's mouth when Qaiyaan entered the room carrying the bulky headset from a nav-grav chair. Behind him, Lisa shouldered a loop of wiring, stringing it along behind her. Qaiyaan set the headset on the countertop. "Captain Kashatok, you're wanted aboard the *Kinship.* Something about your engineer?"

Kashatok's hearts skipped over each other. Next to him, Joy's heartbeat ratcheted up as well. Why hadn't someone called his implant? Eyeing Qaiyaan suspiciously, he tapped below his ear. "*Kinship,* this is the captain. Status update."

Within moments, Doc's voice filled his head. "Captain, you need to come now."

He felt the blood drain from his face. "On my way."

Joy groped for Kashatok's hand. "Gassy?"

The comfort of her touch made him want to stay. Or keep her by his side. But he couldn't. He had to leave her here, not just now, but always. With his other hand, he brushed a loose curl from her forehead. "I have to go."

She squeezed his hand. "Yes, go."

"There's nothing you can do here, anyway," Mek said. "I'll keep you updated."

Kashatok ran a palm over Jhikik's furry head. "Take care of her, Jhik." Then, unable to stop himself, he ran the back of his knuckles down Joy's satiny cheek one last time. "I'll be back."

Staring Mek in the eyes, he reassured himself the doctor had everything in hand before hurrying to the boarding tube. For the first time in over a decade, he sent a prayer to the denaidan god.

Chapter Eleven

With Kashatok gone, Joy shivered, overwhelmed by all that was happening. Gassy might be dying. Would she ever see him again? She held back a sob as the question floated through her mind. She may not *see* anyone *ever again*. Kashatok didn't need a blind mechanic. Remembering his words made her want to vomit.

She kept telling herself the blindness was a temporary side effect, like when she'd received her camera implant; migraines had kept her holed up in her apartment with the shades drawn for days. Yet despite the self-talk, panic pressed down on her chest. Kashatok didn't need a blind mechanic. *Don't let it be permanent.*

Fighting tears, she pressed the heels of her hands against her eyes.

Somewhere to her left, Captain Qaiyaan directed Lisa in positioning some equipment. She could tell when Qaiyaan drew too close because Jhikik stiffened and his teeth clacked. His fur was reassuring and warm against her neck.

Qaiyaan asked, "How're we going to get that creature out of the way?"

"He's not hurting anything. Here, let me," Lisa said. "Joy, I'm going to attach the frequency modulator diodes, all right?"

Joy felt cool hands press the small pads against her temples. Next to her ear, the netorpok vibrated with warning but didn't lunge or bite.

Regaining her composure, Joy asked, "What are you guys doing?"

"When I had the nanites, they were extremely unstable under certain frequencies," Lisa replied. "Especially when we engaged the burn drive."

"Don't worry, Joy." Tovik's voice startled her. "I modified the nav-grav buffers specifically for the nanites. I'll protect you."

Much as she appreciated him trying to help, she wasn't in the mood for his puppy love. "I'll be fine."

"You're still likely to experience some discomfort," Lisa said. "Piggybacking a K-class ship will make things a little rough."

The nanites had settled into a low buzz she could barely hear over Jhikik's purr. For some reason, the influx of data on the *Kinship* had energized the little machines, given them a purpose, and they'd tried to hijack every synapse in her brain to process the information. Since going blind, she hadn't been unconscious so much as *busy*. The mechanic in her had sought to develop a mental "kill switch" of sorts —not anything that would disable the nanites completely, but something to stop their process. She'd succeeded, at least for now, but she had no idea what might bring the machines unexpectedly to life once again.

"Tovik," Qaiyaan said, "get your ass to engineering and finish preparations. Lisa, I need you on the bridge."

Lisa squeezed Joy's hand. "Hang in there."

Footsteps. Then the room was silent. Being blind sucked. "Hello?"

"Don't worry, I'm still here," Mek said. She could hear him moving about on the other side of the room.

Joy stroked Jhikik's shoulder, feeling completely helpless. She longed for Kashatok's reassuring presence. "How long until we burn?"

"Shouldn't be too long. They'll announce it."

Joy took a few more breaths. She needed to focus on something besides her own fear. But the only thing she could think about was the nanites, which made her think about Kashatok. "Can you cure a *carayak*?"

Mek sighed. "No. We never discovered a way to suppress the gene. Then the Termination made continued research unnecessary."

She chewed her lip. "So, there's no hope for him?"

"Not if he's a *carayak*."

"You think he might not be?" She couldn't keep the edge of hope from her voice.

"I can't say. Hopefully, I'll be able to tell from the tissue sample he gave me."

Keeping the tremor from her voice took every ounce of strength she had. "What about his idea about creating an artificial frequency that destroys the nanites?"

The sound of a stool sliding across the floor. Mek finally answered, "The idea has merit, and I've already begun preliminary research. Ionic frequencies are very complex. For mating purposes, they're accompanied by pheromones and hormones within both participants. I'm not sure we'll have time to create and test a procedure before you run out of time."

Her throat tightened. Although Lisa had warned her about the time limit on the nanites, Joy had never imagined the things would take over this fast. She was supposed to have time to prove herself to Kashatok. Not just as a mechanic, but as a woman. Although she'd never thought of herself as attractive before, after he'd kissed her, she'd believed she might be able to tempt him.

If only she'd known.

Footsteps approached the bed. "You can have your pick from our crew—probably either crew—when the time comes."

Just not Kashatok. She turned her head away, needing to grieve in private. "I'm going to try to take a nap. Maybe the blindness will wear off."

"I'm here if you need me." He patted her hand, and she heard his footsteps once again move to the far side of the room.

Her nanites were heating up—an almost prickly sensation inside her head—possibly because of her agitation. God, what was she going to do? As sweet as Tovik was, she felt no desire for the ginger-haired denaidan. None of the men on either ship had ignited her imagination like Kashatok had. A small voice in her head sounded like her mother saying *I told you so*. Her chest tightened.

What if she contacted Mother?

The CEO of the corporation that had created these nanites could probably tell her how to purge them. She'd bet the corp' already had a machine to do it. But contacting her mother without the pirates finding out would be a challenge. How would Joy even locate a comm if she couldn't see it?

You have something stronger than your eyesight. The thought made her heart pound. In engineering, she'd received information from the console from clear across the room. What if she could use the nanites to access a comm? Dare she?

Envisioning the comm's circuitry in her head, she released the brakes on a few of the nanites.

Amidst all the bits of information hammering at her from cyberspace, the comm connection lit up like a firework.

She shifted, wishing she could see what Mek was doing. Could he see her? Would he know if she tried to make a call? And how could she make a call without talking out loud? Would her thoughts translate into words on the other end?

Deciding she had little to lose, she sent a request to connect to her mother's private polycom, adding her own personal identification tracer so Mother would know it was her.

Mother's thin face came into focus as if Joy was looking at a screen. Joy bit down on her lip to keep herself from calling aloud. Mother had never been a nurturing type, but her familiar face provided some comfort.

"Joy? What's wrong with your connection?"

Concentrating, Joy sent, "Mother, I need your help."

"What kind of help?"

Mother could hear her!

The lines on Mother's face deepened as she brought the polycom closer to her face. "And why aren't you on video? Aren't you supposed to be a reporter or some-thing now? You need all the practice you can get."

Joy's relief twisted into the more familiar sensation of self-doubt. "I'm undercover. I've been..." she chose Mek's preferred term, "inoculated with cyber-sensitive nanites from one of Syndicorp's test labs. I need to know how to get rid of them."

"You did what?" Mother's eyes widened. "That technology is still undergoing stage two testing. How did—"

"Never mind that. I don't have much time. Do you know how to destroy the nanites?"

"How did you even find our biotech lab? They told me it was undetectable beneath the gold mine. Well, that will teach you to poke around where you don't belong. I ought to leave you there to learn your lesson."

Joy clenched her teeth. Mother never helped just because Joy asked. "I'm not at a lab. I'm doing an exposé on pirates. Now, are you going to help me or not?"

For the first time Joy could remember, her mother looked truly worried. "Pirates? Are they asking for ransom?"

Shit. I shouldn't have mentioned pirates. "I'm fine. I told you, I'm undercover. They're going to drop me off at the next space port. Please tell me—"

"Don't worry. I'm getting corporate security on this right away, honey. We cannot allow these dirty pirates any leeway. Stay on the line so they can start a trace."

"No!" Joy's eyes flew open, and she sat up, too late realizing she'd spoken aloud.

Jhikik chattered loudly, claws digging into her thigh where he'd latched on after her sudden move. She swore Mek's concerned face flashed before her eyes.

The doctor's voice spoke from her right. "Are you hurt?"

Joy couldn't answer. Images were flickering through her brain; Mother, Jhikik, comm circuitry, Mek. Her head throbbed as if she was having a root canal done on her brain. What the fuck was going on? She gritted her teeth and focused on one command. *Kill switch!*

Kashatok crossed the boarding tube in a single stride and passed through the empty cargo bay as if he was flying. Where the hell were his guards? If there was one thing being in the cartel had taught him, it was never to expose your back, not even to a fellow pirate. He had some words for Aleknagik the next time he saw him.

As he passed the weapons locker, he thought of Joy, blind and unprotected on the other ship. Yet jealous as he was of Tovik, the kid would watch out for her and his gut told him she was better off with a doctor who knew what he was doing. *Damn her for taking the nanites, anyway.* He'd known the Syndicorp tech could be nothing but trouble. Right now, he had to think about Gassy.

He took the corner into the *Kinship's* med bay so fast, he had to hold the doorframe as he entered. The room stank of disinfectant and blood. His gaze scoured the room, finding the old engineer alone and lying beneath the sterility shield just as before. "Gassy?"

Gassy opened his eyes. "Hey."

Settling on the tall stool beside the bed, Kashatok assessed the steady heartbeats on the vitals monitor. He wasn't a doctor, but the lines and numbers there seemed the same as before. "Where's Doc? I got a call that something was wrong."

"I heard a bunch of noise earlier, but no one came in here."

The back of Kashatok's neck prickled with ionic awareness and a sickening weight settled in his gut. Someone stood behind him. He rose slowly and turned toward the door.

Aleknagik stood just inside, legs wide and arms crossed. In the corridor behind him, Doc and Manopup held pulse pistols.

"What the fuck?" Kashatok ground out, blood running cold.

"Crew's voted you out," Aleknagik said.

Behind him, Gassy coughed wetly. "Why didn't I hear about a vote?"

"This is mutiny." Kashatok took a step forward, halting when the two men in the corridor trained their pistols on him. "Aleknagik, tell them to stand down."

"This isn't a trooper ship, Captain." Aleknagik raised one eyebrow. "We're pirates. We all have a share. We voted. You betrayed us by breaking your own rule."

"You son of a rakwiji whore." Kashatok clenched his hands. "You had as much part in hiring her as I did."

"Yep. And I'll bring her aboard again, just as soon as the nanites are done with her." Aleknagik grinned. "Different captain, different rules."

Kashatok jutted out his chin. His first mate had nothing good planned, but perhaps the rest of the crew could see reason. "She can't be your mechanic. She's blind. Useless."

"Nobody's useless." Aleknagik's grin widened, and he placed a palm to his chest. "Besides, she's crew, wounded in the line of duty. We take care of our own." The first mate flicked a glance over his shoulder at his men. "Right?"

"I am sure she will find new positions among the crew."

Manopup's tentacles writhed. Someone Kashatok couldn't see snickered from the corridor.

"I'll kill you all first." Kashatok took another step.

A pulse blast hit him in the shoulder, spinning him around. Men moved into the room. Gassy called out from the bed. "Stop!"

The cold, hard point of a pulse pistol jammed into Kashatok's lower spine. He struggled against rough hands. The pulse blast had left his entire arm unresponsive. Aleknagik cinched a zip tie around his wrists. "We need you alive—at least for now. But if you do or say anything we don't like, Gassy gets it."

At the bedside, Manopup held his pistol loosely trained on the engineer.

"Doc," Kashatok twisted, boring his gaze into the denaidan who'd remained in the corridor. "How can you do this?"

Doc shrugged without meeting Kashatok's eyes. "The crew voted."

"To the brig." Aleknagik shoved Kashatok toward the doorway, sending a flare of pain through his shoulder.

"The *Hardship* won't hand Joy over once they find out

what you've done," Kashatok said as he moved down the corridor.

They rounded a corner and Aleknagik yanked Kashatok close to hiss in his ear. "You think I really give an *anaq* about the female? I have a fresh piece of ass in every port." Aleknagik jammed a hand between Kashatok's shoulder blades and sent him reeling into the tiny room used for a brig. "The men want her aboard. And a good captain listens to his men." The door shield engaged with a subliminal crackle. "It's about time the *Kinship* had a worthy captain."

"You will never be worthy," Kashatok righted himself and stood tall in front of the glimmering shield, glaring at his first mate. How could his crew do this? He'd never been tight with his men, but they'd always respected his authority. *Or wanted your cartel connections.* After the most recent failed job, they obviously wanted him gone. *Uminaq,* a drink would go down well right now.

Aleknagik leaned forward, his face millimeters from the door shield. "Tell you what. Make this easy for me, and I won't insist on bringing the female over."

Kashatok grit his teeth and clenched his fists. "You want me to hand over my ship."

Nodding his shaggy head, the first mate looked as pleased as an ohn-cat who'd drunk all the cream. "Just keep things friendly with the *Hardship* until they cut us free."

"And what happens to me when this is over?"

"Hm. The punishment for bringing a woman on board is space-locking, I believe?" Aleknagik grinned. "But if you're good, I'll try to make sure we're within hailing distance of the *Hardship* when we do it. Perhaps they'll pick you up."

Chignik's voice came over the ship-wide comm. "We burn in six. Stand ready."

"The captain's needed on the bridge." Aleknagik shot Kashatok a mocking glance. "Oh, that's right. That's me."

With that, he turned on his heel and disappeared down the hall.

Still reeling from the pulse shot and burning with fury at his crew, Kashatok stabilized himself for burn.

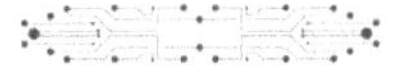

Joy had been through countless burn cycles in her life, but never one that'd felt like this. Even with the nav-grav buffer, the burn drive emitted a frequency that drove her nanites crazy. The little machines seemed to spin and swarm like insects looking for a hive. Whenever the machines touched each other, they arced, creating strange flavors in her mouth, making her skin heat and cool, speeding or slowing her heartbeat. Her camera flickered on and off in a random pattern that felt like it would send her into a seizure at any moment. How had Lisa survived this chaos?

Clutching the bedsheets at her sides, she squeezed her eyes shut and concentrated on the 3D layered structure of one of the nanites along her optic nerve. The things were acting like the actuators in a bio-responsive holo-suite she'd once repaired. Sure enough, the gel-metal composite in the one she examined was flexing in response to the ship's burn frequency. What if she lined up its molecular structure with a second nanite? Could she alter the frequency receptors?

The two tiny machines clamped onto each other like puzzle pieces, calming immediately.

She lined more nanites up. Behind her closed eyelids, steady pinpricks of light, like illuminated micro-pixels, appeared. Opening her eyes, she was disheartened to see only the same colorless pixels. She needed more nanites engaged.

There were thousands, however—hundreds of thousands. She'd barely begun and was already sagging with fatigue.

As suddenly as it had begun, the burn frequency cut off. The nanites slowed. Settled. Joy's head throbbed as if someone had taken a jackhammer to it, but she let out a gusty sigh of relief. She had some time to recover.

A voice from the comm pierced through her headache. "Mek, how's our passenger?"

"Joy, you still with us?" Mek asked.

"Working on it," she mumbled, surprised she still had control of her tongue.

"Excellent." His hand patted hers. "The buffers appear to work, Captain."

"That's good news. But I have some not-so-good. Troopers somehow picked up our trail as we left the asteroid belt," Qaiyaan said. "We need to burn again immediately."

Joy couldn't be sure, but she thought she heard herself whimper. For a moment, she actually yearned for the troopers to catch them; she was the daughter of the CEO, after all. It would be like running home to Mother. Then again, the troopers hadn't paused to talk when they'd approached the slave ship before trying to blast the *Kinship* out of space. She bit her lip, trying to be brave. The only way to survive this was to keep going.

Mek moved quietly beside her, checking monitors. "You heard him. Need anything before we go?"

The nanites were relaying her medical information from the sensors. Elevated blood pressure, high levels of cortisol, increased respiration. Would another burn cycle kill her? She didn't think so. "Just get it over with."

"Ready when you are, Captain."

Her nanites jolted once more into chaos.

Chapter Twelve

The first burn was short, exactly what Kashatok expected for a piggyback. Arm and hand still tingling from the pulse shot to his shoulder, he dropped his ionic shielding and began prying open the door's force shield control panel. He didn't trust Aleknagik to keep any promises, not about keeping Kashatok alive, and certainly not about Joy. Getting out of this cell was top priority.

Suddenly, his balance was yanked out from under him and his vision went blurry. He staggered sideways, hitting his head on the wall. His knees buckled and his stomach heaved as space folded in on itself and the ships' frequencies adjusted to the new location. A second burn? *Ellam Cua,* why hadn't anyone announced it?

Raising his ionic shield, he sat on the floor with his back pressed into a corner, head throbbing as he rode out the burn. Such a quick cycle could only mean trouble. Was Joy all right? Was the *Hardship's* crew onto Aleknagik? Had the troopers managed to catch their trail? He loathed not knowing; not being able to make decisions.

When the burn ended, Kashatok crawled to the door's force shield and peered down the hall through the glittering curtain. "Hey! Someone?"

A cut from his scalp trickled down his forehead, dripping blood into his eye. He swiped at the sting, hand coming away turquoise. A soft chirp to his left drew his attention.

"Jhikik?"

Another chirp rose from a floor vent no bigger than his palm. He crawled over to find two glistening eyes staring up at him through the grate. Poor little guy. The netorpok generally sat on his shoulder during burn, wrapped in Kashatok's ionic shield. Or cuddled up to Joy. Why wasn't Jhikik with her? Had Mek or Qaiyaan chased him away? Anger simmered in the pit of Kashatok's stomach.

Siphoning what little ionic power he could dredge up past his nausea, Kashatok yanked the grate free.

Jhikik squeezed through the opening, tail clutching a sock behind him. He scampered up Kashatok's arm and nestled against his neck, trembling.

"Caught you unaware, too? Why are you here?" He stroked the creature's downy head.

The tip of the netorpok's tail raised the sock in front of Kashatok's face like a peace flag, the fabric full of shredded holes. Jhikik chirped again.

Guilt swept through him. *"Anaq.* You're hungry, huh?"

When was the last time he'd fed his pet? Hell, when was the last time *he'd* eaten? Too much had been happening too fast. Legs unsteady, he rose, praying there wouldn't be a third burn without warning. At the door, he resumed efforts on the shield control panel. A shadow of movement from the corridor made him thrust his hands into his pockets a heartbeat before someone rounded the corner from the cargo bay.

Chignik. The denaidan carried an open bottle of rum, his multiple braids hanging limp and a line of blood darkening his chin. "Hey, Cap."

Kashatok glared at the man, betrayal washing through him all over again. He crossed his arms. "You going to tell me what's going on?"

Chignik took a long swallow from the bottle, swaying just a little. "I voted against it, just so you know."

Exhaling slowly, Kashatok met his crewman's bleary gaze. Not all his men had mutinied. There was still hope. "Get me out of here, then."

"Can't." Chignik shook his head. "Aleknagik revoked my codes."

Kashatok closed his eyes a moment, previous hope stretching thin. "Anyone else on our side?"

"Gassy, but he's not good for much right now. Ekwok maybe." Chignik took another drink. "He abstained from the vote. Cooper kept saying he didn't like it, but in the end, he voted with Aleknagik."

Kashatok paced in front of the door, legs still unsteady. Aleknagik had always been good at dominating the crew. It was part of what made him a good first mate, or so Kashatok'd believed. "Why'd we do a second burn so soon?"

"Troopers caught our signature and were hot on our tail. Aleknagik says they're after your woman."

Kashatok paused, only halfway registering that Chignik had referred to Joy as his woman. "Why would they be after her?"

Chignik blinked slowly, lids slightly out of synch. "Her mother broadcast a reward. Moore caught it on one of the Syndicorp channels he was monitoring from the slave ship."

"Mother?" For some reason, he hadn't pictured Joy with family, let alone a mother with enough power to put an entire trooper ship into action.

"She's offering one point five mil to anyone who leads the authorities to Joy's kidnappers."

Kashatok clenched his fists. Joy's family assumed she'd been kidnapped. But what kind of family could offer a one point five mil reward? That was an *anaq*-load of creds, worth the crew's total shares for an entire solar year at least. "Who the fuck is she?"

"Syndicorp's CEO. Joy's last name is Mulholland-Aird." The words felt like pulse blasts coming from Chignik's lips, stunning Kashatok for a few heartbeats.

He ran a hand down his beard. He'd never bothered with last names among his crew. "That's ridiculous. It can't be."

Shrugging, Chignik dabbed at his bloody lip with the back of his hand. "She called Joy by name and had a picture of her with longer hair."

Kashatok put one hand against the wall to steady himself. Syndicorp? How was that possible? And how did that play into Joy seeking a spot on his crew? Had she been after the nanites all along? Fuck, he needed a drink. He was about to reach through the damned door shield and rip the bottle from Chignik's fingers.

Next to Kashatok's ear, Jhikik purred softly. Kashatok absently rubbed the soft fur under his pet's chin. There had to be a good explanation. Joy might've disguised herself to get on board, but she wasn't a very good liar. She'd told the truth about her name; he'd chosen to mishear it. When Gassy first mentioned the nanites, she'd been completely clueless. And she'd flat-out told him she wasn't a Syndicorp spy. He believed her.

But the others didn't and now she was alone on the other ship. *Uminaq*! He straightened, staring helplessly through the door shield. "What did Captain Qaiyaan say?"

Chignik shook his head. "Don't think he knows. Aleknagik wants to keep it that way." A queasy look came over the big man's bearded face. "He says after we have our fun, the ransom is ours."

Both of Kashatok's hearts slammed against his ribs. There was absolutely zero chance Aleknagik would honor his promise of leaving her aboard the *Hardship* now—if he'd ever intended to in the first place. "You can't let Aleknagik and his men get their hands on Joy." His insides tightened as he thought of her at Aleknagik's mercy. What would Qaiyaan and his crew do once they found out she was Syndicorp? At least they valued her for the nanites. "Think you can get a message to her?"

"Like I said, my access codes are no good," Chignik said. "But maybe I can sweet talk Ekwok into doing it. Or get Gassy up long enough to send one."

"You have to try."

Chignik turned to go and Jhikik chirped again, tail in a stranglehold around Kashatok's neck. *Still hungry.* At least he could try to get Jhik some food.

"Chignik?" Kashatok called after him. "Open the hydroponic gate in my cabin so Jhikik can eat?"

None of the crewmen liked the netorpok, but Chignik looked over his shoulder and nodded. He disappeared unsteadily around the corner, leaving Kashatok and Jhikik alone once more.

Kashatok pulled Jhikik off his shoulder and placed him near the grate. "Feast while you can. Aleknagik'll probably toss you out the airlock with me."

Jhikik chirped with alarm, tail clinging to Kashatok's wrist.

For the first time in a long time, Kashatok realized he might regret dying. He'd probably never see Joy again. The thought created a void inside him that wanted to fold in on itself. "I know, buddy. Go back to her if you can."

Then an idea occurred to him—maybe Jhikik could go back. He could carry a message to her. Kashatok patted his pockets and glanced around the barren room as if he might find something to write on. Or with, for that matter. Nothing. Blinking, he wiped a dribble of blood from his forehead with his sleeve, absently noting the stark turquoise blood against the white fabric. He may not be able to write a message, but he could send a warning.

Tearing a strip of fabric from the shirt's hem, he dabbed it against his forehead, then tied it like a collar around a squirming Jhikik's neck. *Anaq,* did she even know his blood was turquoise? As if she could even see it. She was blind for *Ellam Cua's* sake. Yet it wasn't as if he had any other options. Perhaps Mek would notice the collar and say something.

Nudging his companion toward the grate, he said, "Take it to Joy."

The netorpok looked over his shoulder at Kashatok for a moment, then disappeared down the black hole.

Kashatok prayed like hell the creature didn't get distracted by the open hydroponics cage.

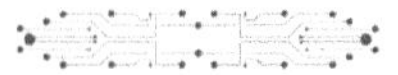

The burn ended, and Joy sagged with mental relief. She'd aligned enough nanites that the tiny machines could continue stacking on their own, like a chain reaction. She'd always had a knack for mechanics, but the nanites were painting a more rounded picture of the ship's systems than she'd ever imagined possible. She could sense the slight variation in the gravity system Tovik had chattered to her about. Knew Mek's centrifuge needed balancing. Next to her, she detected the report on her biological systems from the scanner Mek held close to her ear.

But the volume of information was also exhausting, and it took everything she had left to shut it out. She'd never worked so hard in her life. Deep in her chest, she trembled with fatigue, her eyes glued shut as if each lid weighed a thousand pounds. Even her hands ached as if she'd been wielding a wrench for hours on end. She could fall asleep for days and still not feel rested, yet a small part of her refused to let go of consciousness in case the nanites decided to get frisky once again. If they returned to chaos, she'd drown under the onslaught.

The emanations from Mek's scanner changed frequencies, and she groaned.

"How're you doing, Joy?"

"Can you not do that?"

"Sorry." The scanner ceased, but Mek jabbed her arm for what felt like the millionth time. "I'm taking another sample."

Something beeped, and the nanites jittered like toddlers refusing to take a nap. She heard Mek shuffling around the room as she lapsed back into semi-consciousness.

"I have some good news for Captain Kashatok about his DNA test." The doctor's voice startled her alert.

Then she realized what he'd said. *News for Kashatok.* As if responding to her curiosity, her nanites sifted through the nearby information, returning the DNA results; Kashatok did not have *carayak* disorder. Her eyes flew open. Bright whiteness sliced into her brain, and she slammed her lids shut again. *What the hell?*

She must've made a noise, because Mek asked, "Joy?"

Carefully slitting her right eye, her heart fell. Black void. Shutting it, she cracked open her left lid and winced as a crescent of light filtered through her lashes. *Filters,* she ordered out of habit. Her camera responded by dialing down the lens receptors. The light became bearable. She opened her eye the rest of the way.

The brilliant overhead light of the med bay came into focus amidst the grooved ceiling panels. Her heart skipped several beats, and excitement filled her limbs. She wasn't blind! Then everything grew fuzzy again, and she wanted to cry before she realized things were fuzzy because she was crying. She lifted her hands and pressed away the tears, letting out a sobbing laugh. "I can see!"

She turned her head to find Mek beside the bed, a grin splitting his face. "That's wonderful news! I have to admit, I was worried your optic nerve was permanently damaged."

He grabbed a scanner and pressed it to her temple. She winced as the nanites did their dance, but bore it. This was worth the discomfort.

Mek's face grew serious. "You're sure you can see? Your optic nerves are still non-responsive."

She closed and opened her left eye, confirming her suspicion. "It's my camera."

Even as she said it, she bit her lip. She was still blind. Her camera would never be the same as her real vision. For one thing, it was only in one eye. For another, extended use brought on a migraine.

"Let me run some tests." Mek pursed his lips as if mulling something over, then turned to his workstation.

Joy knew she should turn the camera off. Reserve using it for when it was needed. But she was too relieved and excited. "I want to tell Kashatok."

"I just tried to call him. His crew says he's occupied, but he'll call back as soon as he can."

She fumbled with the nav-grav harness securing her chest and legs to the cot. Her fingers didn't want to obey commands for fine motor skills.

Mek gave her a warning frown over his shoulder. "Slow down, Joy. More than just your eyesight is being affected."

"I'm tired of lying here helpless." Inside her head, the nanites responded to her agitation and excitement with another monster headache.

A tiny weight landed on her legs, and she glanced down to find Jhikik scampering toward her.

"Jhikik! I can see!" She spotted a rag tied around his neck. He'd never worn a collar before. Reaching out, she tried unsuccessfully to untie the knot. "Who did this?"

"What?" Mek asked.

"There's something tied on him. Can you help get it off?"

Mek raised an eyebrow. "I don't think he likes me."

She rubbed behind Jhikik's ears. "Jhikik, will you let the doctor get that thing off you? For me?"

Jhikik purred, closing his dark eyes.

Mek sighed and moved closer. Jhikik's purring turned to warning clicks, but he allowed the doctor to worry the knot free. Mek held up the white and turquoise scrap of cloth. "This appears to be blood."

A chill settled into Joy's veins. She took the cloth from him, fingering the soft pirelux fabric. Kashatok's shirt had been made of the same material. "Try to call Kashatok again."

Mek nodded and walked over to the comm. "This is Mekoryuk on the *Hardship*. I need to speak to Captain Kashatok immediately."

Aleknagik's voice came back. "Is it about the female? I can give him a message."

Joy's hackles rose. Kashatok had warned her his crew was dangerous, but referring to her as if she was some sort of livestock rankled her. Jhikik climbed to her shoulder and clicked his teeth in agreement.

Mek said, "This is for Kashatok's ears only."

A pause. "I'll see if I can free him up. We'll call back."

Joy met Mek's eyes across the med bay. Something wasn't right. "Try his cochlear implant."

"You have the code?" he asked.

She didn't, but her nanites could get it. In fact, she could probably use her nanites to call him directly. "Let me try my nanites."

"No!" The urgency in Mek's voice stalled her. "Encouraging them at this stage could be dangerous. Lisa only escaped their control with her brother's help."

"But Kashatok may be in trouble." She held up the rag.

"That's different from trying to command them."

The comm came to life once again, this time with Qaiyaan's voice. "Mek, can you leave your patient for a few minutes and come to the bridge? We've just received some intel and need to talk."

Joy swung her legs over the edge of the bed. "I'm coming, too."

The comm was still open, because Qaiyaan replied, "Crew only, Joy. Hang tight. We'll only be a few minutes."

Mek held up a palm. "Stay and rest. I'll get the code from Qaiyaan and when I get back, we'll call Kashatok."

She settled back against the pillow, but inside, she knew something was very wrong. Jhikik knew it too, pacing the mattress beside her as if asking her what she was waiting for. Kashatok needed her and there was no time to waste. She could feel it in her gut. In her nanites.

Once the doctor was gone, Jhikik hopped down and, with a quick glance over his shoulder, disappeared through the door. She swore she heard him say, *Come on.*

She swung her legs over the edge of the bed. The nanites were under control. It wasn't far to the boarding tube. She would just pop over with Jhikik, make sure Kashatok was okay, and come back.

Except her legs refused to support her. No way was she walking out of here right now. She slumped back to the cot. *Fuck.* If she could just reach Kashatok's implant, she'd feel better. The nanites could do it in mere seconds. She winked her camera eye, testing the micro-computers now embedded in the interface. She appeared to have full control. Surely one quick search and a comm call wouldn't be harmful? She'd managed with Mother easily enough.

Closing her eyes, she opened an interface to the comm.

A stream of information surged through her senses. She throttled the flow, focusing on what she wanted. Kashatok's implant. *There it is.* Easy as she'd imagined. But some kind of firewall stood between her and the connection. An intentional block within the *Kinship's* comm array. She recognized that signature from her work on the ship's systems.

He was in the brig.

What the hell?

"Mek!" she called out, hoping he could hear her from here. She had to tell him. Now. Realizing she was still connected to the comm system, she opened a line to the bridge.

The men were talking loudly, Tovik's voice overriding the others. "Kashatok probably *did* kidnap her!"

A sickening sensation filled her throat. They were talking about her. She should've known when Qaiyaan called for crew only. She concentrated harder, trying to make out who was saying what.

"Whatever the case," said Qaiyaan's deeper tone, "we can't just let her run around free if she's Syndicorp."

She stiffened, breath catching. How could they know?

"One point five mil creds is a lot," said a voice she wasn't as familiar with, but she thought might be the first mate. "If she's not matable, we should turn her in and collect."

"We can't let her go," Lisa said. "It'd compromise our search for the lab if her mother finds out about the nanites. My brother…"

But Joy was barely listening. The pirates knew because of Mother. With a surge of adrenaline, Joy found herself on her feet. Trembling, but upright.

Tovik's voice cracked loudly over the connection, "Are you suggesting we kill her?"

Holy shit, they were coming to murder her. Throat too tight to swallow, she cut the connection, not trusting her command of the nanites enough to use the comm and her camera at the same time. Forcing her feet to take one step after another, she stumbled to the door, gaining more motor control the closer she got to the boarding tube. Did the men on the *Kinship* know? Did Kashatok? Was he in the brig because of her? If she'd learned anything during her time on Kashatok's ship, it was that denaidans hated Syndicorp more than anything else in existence. These pirates would torture and kill her before ransoming her lifeless corpse back to her mother and the corp'.

Not Kashatok. He'd scared her at first, but she'd come to recognize the good behind his drunken, savage appearance. He'd tried to shield her, cared for her, made her believe he saw something special in her. Kashatok was the one man among all these pirates who might actually protect her, Syndicorp or not.

But first, she had to get him free.

Chapter Thirteen

Joy gripped the edge of the boarding tube and peered into the *Kinship's* cargo bay. At the back of the dimly lit cavern, Moore sat with his wiry back to her across one of the cargo crates from Ekwok. Without being sure if they knew about Mother, she couldn't risk being seen. But how was she going to get past them? They were obviously guards, and Ekwok had a clear view of the boarding tube.

The tawny-haired denaidan glanced up, then jerked his gaze back to his cards.

She trembled, bracing herself against the edge of the tube. He'd seen her. But a moment passed, then another, and he continued staring at his hand. Perhaps he had poor eyesight? She edged onto the deck and hugged the outer wall, hurrying toward the angular shuttle sitting in the starboard bay. Ducking behind the rear landing strut, she paused, leaning against the hard metal and panting. The nanites were going wild from adrenaline. She squeezed her eyes shut, imagining herself holding a spanner, tightening her hold on the little machines. The kill switch was not a preferable option; without the nanites, she'd be blind, and she wasn't quite that familiar with the *Kinship's* layout.

The single-cell brig lay around the corner just past the escape pods. Would there be more guards there? She was unarmed, unstable, completely unprepared—what the hell had she been thinking, fleeing the *Hardship* without a plan? What had she been thinking when she decided to go undercover in the first place? Now she was trapped between two pirate crews with nowhere to flee except the vacuum of space.

Next to her, the shuttle door stood open as if inviting her to try. Not that she'd get anywhere that way; the *Kinship* would never open the landing bay door, and the umbilical to the ship's main diagnostic system was still connected to the shuttle's belly. But there were tools inside the shuttle. Carrying something as a weapon would make her feel better.

She crept on board, crouching so she couldn't be seen through the windows. On her hands and knees, she rifled through the emergency locker, tucking a screw-driver into her back pocket and gripping a large span-ner. She turned to exit, but her gaze caught the open panel of the shuttle's micro-drive. She'd been calibrating the power coil's coolant system before they encountered the slave ship. If she adjusted it toward the negative end and engaged the shuttle's life support, the coil would overheat in about five minutes, sending an alarm to the console in main engineering. A very loud alarm.

That could be enough diversion to get her to the brig undetected. Without an engineer, the crew'd scramble to figure out what the noise was. On the other hand, if someone didn't figure out what was wrong and shut it down, the shuttle's innards would experience a melt-down. Possibly explode.

By then, you'll have Kashatok free. The brig's door controls should be a piece of cake to override using the spanner in her pocket. Together, they'd return to the shuttle and shut the power coil down. Hell, maybe they could actu-ally use the shuttle to escape.

Sucky plan, but it was all she had.

She made the adjustment and crept outside, waiting nervously near the shuttle's pointed nose.

Heartbeat loud in her ears, she watched the mouth of the corridor expectantly for what felt like hours. The nanites seemed to surge in time with her pulse, making her camera's focus go in and out. She shut her eyes against the disorienting sensation, but only for a moment. She couldn't afford to be blind if someone came around the corner and spotted her.

Finally, a rolling wail echoed through the bay. She counted to ten before peeking around the nose. The guards had risen, and she caught sight of Ekwok disappearing into the far corridor. Moore remained at the makeshift table with his back to her.

She slipped from behind the shuttle and darted toward the door to the brig, sure she'd feel the bite of a pulse blast at any moment. Clearing the corner, she breathed a sigh of relief and took the last few steps. The door's force shield glimmered, making her camera's auto-filters roll through several settings before stabilizing. Once she could see again, she peered through the shield to meet Kashatok's furious gaze.

The alarm bell rolling through the ship was a perfect accompaniment to the confusion coursing through Kashatok's system. Joy was here, looking at him. His hearts warred with conflicting emotions. Joy could see again? Had she received his warning? If she had, why was she here? And the thing he really didn't want to know—was she actually a Syndicorp spy?

He said the only thing he could think of. "You shouldn't be here."

She jimmied the door's control panel loose and applied the spanner to the mechanism. "I got your message."

He glanced to the corner where Jhikik hunkered over a naujiar branch he'd dragged up the vent a few minutes earlier. "The collar was supposed to be a warning, not an invitation."

The glittering force shield sputtered and dissipated. Joy dropped the spanner and flung herself into his arms. "Did they hurt you?"

Any anger he may have been trying to summon vanished. She felt so good, so right. He'd lived aloof for so long, he'd forgotten the simple pleasure of being touched. Stealing a moment to return her embrace, he breathed deeply against her hair, filling himself with her essence.

The alarm cut off as suddenly as it began. He pushed her away. "You're in danger. Go back right now."

"I can't." She was trembling, her liquid brown eyes tense. "Kashatok, there's something I need to tell you."

He wrapped one hand around her arm and pulled her from the brig, listening intently for approaching footsteps before turning toward the cargo bay. "You're Syndicorp, I know."

She stiffened. "I'm not, though."

He took a deep breath. He didn't have time to argue. Whatever was occupying the crew wasn't likely to last. Looking over his shoulder, he said, "Either way, you're not safe here."

"Neither are you. They locked you up because of me, didn't they? Are they planning to kill you?"

He continued pulling her forward. "We don't have time to stand here and—"

A pulse blast whizzed past his shoulder. He grabbed Joy around the waist and dashed into the cavernous bay, sidestepping around the corner. Setting her down, he scanned the open space for other attackers. The shuttle blocked his view of the boarding tube, but the rest of the bay appeared empty.

He looked at Joy's empty hands. "Did you happen to bring a weapon?"

She cringed. "I dropped the spanner back there." Pulling a small screwdriver from her back pocket, she held it out. "This is all I have."

"*Uminaq!*" Ignoring the screwdriver, he turned to face the mouth of the corridor. Standing between their attacker and Joy, he could protect them from one pulse blast with his ionic shielding. He prayed no one crept up on them from behind the shuttle. Joy moved in close, her warmth reassuring against his back.

Aleknagik's shaggy head poked around the corner several feet away, followed by a pistol leveled at Kashatok's chest. The mutinous first mate stepped into view as casually as if he were saying hello. "I wondered if I might find you together. Good to see our little female in working order again."

"Leave her alone." Kashatok balled his fists, daring the man to come within range.

"Can't. Turns out you not only brought a female on board but a Syndicorp spy. Captain Qaiyaan's eager to talk to the lady in question."

Kashatok maintained his shield, glancing desperately around the big bay. If both crews knew Joy was Syndicorp, neither ship was safe for her. But there was a third option. "Let us take the shuttle, and I'll relinquish the *Kinship*. Yours, free and clear."

Joy's breath fanned over his shoulder blade. "Kashatok, I don't…"

A new voice echoed through the cargo bay from the comm. "Captain, I'm detecting troopers on long-range sensors. They've found us again."

Aleknagik extended his free hand forward. "Tell you what. Hand her over and I'll let *you* take the shuttle."

"Fuck you." Kashatok snarled.

The sound of raised voices echoed from beyond the shuttle, Tovik's youthful voice carrying through the bay. "I don't think you understand how serious this is. Just let me help look for her. She's probably in engineering."

"Captain gave me direct orders not to allow you on board. Now get off our ship." Moore's gravelly retort left no question about whose side he was on.

Aleknagik's nose flared. "Sounds like she has that little punk as duped as you are, Kashatok."

The comm crackled again. "Troopers are coming in fast. The *Hardship* says we have to burn in three."

"She's not a spy," Kashatok said, putting as much surety behind his words as he could muster.

"Are you sure?" Aleknagik tilted his head, eyes narrowed. "The troopers have tracked us through two burns."

Tracking a ship through burn was difficult, to say the least; the frequency alignments that allowed a burn drive to fold space were very precise. A spy on board the *Kinship* would make the troopers' arrival much more plausible. Deep inside, Kashatok fought to contain his doubts. Was Joy responsible?

More arguing echoed from the other side of the shuttle. Tovik sputtered, "If she's not buffered when we burn, the nanites could kill her!"

"You hear that?" Aleknagik tilted his head toward the shuttle. "We don't have much time. Step aside, and I'll make sure she gets stabilized. We'd all prefer to keep her..." His teeth flashed in a grotesque leer. "Functioning."

Joy's fingertips dug into Kashatok's sides, and he could sense her heart racing. Every instinct told him to protect her. But what could he do?

"Two minutes," the comm announced.

Kashatok ground his teeth. Even if Joy ran, she'd never get herself positioned into a nav-grav seat in time. Burning was no longer an option—they had to stand and fight. He took a deep breath and shouted, "Battle stations!"

From the far end of the bay, Ekwok appeared from the opposite corridor. He stopped and gaped. "Captain?"

At Kashatok's back, Joy's warmth faded. She must've moved. If she wasn't directly behind him, she'd be vulnerable to a blast from the pulse pistol. "Joy, stay close." He took a step backward without taking his gaze off Aleknagik. Speaking loud enough to be heard throughout the bay, he said, "Are we going to run like scared dogs forever? We stand here with two ships. Two crews. It's time to stand and fight!"

Aleknagik aimed the pistol barrel at Kashatok's head.

Kashatok focused all his power to the front of his ionic shield.

The comm announced, "One minute to burn."

It was too late. Too late for everything. Kashatok's entire sorry existence flickered before his eyes. Yet damned if he wouldn't go down fighting. He coiled himself to pounce as a clunk and a hiss came from behind him, followed by a rush of stale air.

Joy's hand gripped the back of his waistband, yanking him backward through the narrow opening of an escape pod. He sensed a pulse blast headed his direction. Reality became slow motion as he grappled for the pod door. His fingers wrapped around the door's airlock wheel. A pulse blast struck him straight in the chest, knocking him off his feet.

And his world went black.

CHAPTER FOURTEEN

Kashatok opened gritty eyes, his head pillowed against warm skin. Above him, a brushed metal ceiling glowed with ambient light. Green and amber alerts blinked somewhere in his peripheral vision. His ribcage felt like he'd been used as a punching bag. He let out a slow breath, his ionic senses detecting a beating heart to his left just as a cool hand cupped his cheek.

Joy's face moved into his line of sight. "Kashatok? Are you awake?"

For a moment, he simply drank in her smooth olive complexion, the short dark ringlets surrounding her face, the liquid quality of her eyes. "What happened?"

A shiver coursed through her, and he realized his head was cradled on her lap. "You grabbed the escape pod's door handle just as you were shot. The blow shoved you backward, slamming the hatch shut. I hit the seal and ejected."

He remembered now; they'd been within seconds of burn. An escape pod caught by the edge of a ship's burn frequency was either pulled along, torn apart, or flung into a random sector of space. A pod could even end up in another galaxy, although no one had ever returned to prove it true. "What are our coordinates?"

She shook her head. "I can't tell."

Then he realized she wasn't looking at him. She wasn't looking at anything. His stomach tightened, and he reached up to caress her velvety cheek with the back of one hand. "Are you blind again?"

Her eyes performed a hard, slow blink, then she met his gaze. "My eyes can't see, but my camera can. I get a headache using it for too long. And I can only use the nanites for one thing at a time. I was reading the ship's systems just now."

He wasn't sure whether to be grateful or worried. "We have to get you to a doctor."

Although he wanted to remain in the comfort of her lap, he sat up, one hand pressed against his bruised ribs. The pod was literally that: a metal hexagon with passenger seats on four sides and a viewport with a rudimentary control panel on the fifth. Sprawled on the floor, he took up the entire space. No wonder he'd been on her lap.

On hands and knees, he moved to the panel, muscles still spasming with the aftershocks from the deflected pulse blast, and knelt in front of the controls. A green light next to the comm indicated the emergency beacon had automatically engaged after they ejected. Life support was also green. The navigation system blinked amber, unable to correlate their current position with any locations in its databank. Not that it really mattered; the pod had the maneuverability of a rowboat.

Swallowing, he did a sensor scan of the surrounding space. Emptiness. "How long was I out?"

Joy scooted over and knelt behind him, one soft breast brushing his shoulder as she leaned forward to view the panel. "A few hours, I think."

A few hours and no one had responded to their emergency beacon. This did not bode well. He relaxed onto his heels.

Joy settled back to make room, her breath fanning his shoulder. "Where are we?"

"Nowhere."

For long moments, they both stared at the blinking control panel. They were out of tools and out of alternatives.

"How long can we survive in the pod?" she whispered.

He'd been asking himself the same thing. Turning, he sat cross-legged to face her. "It's designed to keep three or four crewmen alive a few days. We might have a week with only two of us."

She grimaced. "And you didn't detect any nearby systems?"

He shook his head. He could feel her heartbeat racing and smell her warm citrus scent filling the pod's small space. Watching as she chewed her bottom lip in that distracting fashion of hers, he was filled with the desire to run his thumb across her mouth, to press inside and feel her teeth and tongue and…

How could he be thinking about these things when they were facing imminent death? He forced himself to look away.

"Are we going to die out here?" she asked.

He swallowed. No sense hiding the truth. They were in this together. "Probably."

She inhaled and blew it out in a long breath. "Then I have a final request."

He dragged his gaze back to her face, meeting her liquid brown eyes. The intensity there was shocking, sending sparks directly into his bloodstream.

She licked her lips, leaving them moist and rosy. "Make love to me."

Her request about knocked him flat. What was she thinking? She knew he couldn't. Yet her heartbeat fluttered, her breathing quickened, and her body temperature rose in what could only be classified as arousal. *Uminaq,* even her scent told him she wanted him at least as much as he wanted her. "You know I can't."

"I think you can. Mek said he had good news for you before everything fell apart. I'm pretty sure it was the results of your DNA test." She smiled tremulously. "You're not a *carayak.*"

Her words made no sense. For almost two decades, he'd lived without sex, defining himself as a monster. Mek's test had to be wrong. *Wrong or right, you still can't be with her.* She was human. He was denaidan. "*Carayak* or not, I can't be with you."

She seemed to shrink, her shoulders drawing up. "You don't want me?"

"Of course I want you!" The words were out before he could rein them in. Even his cock surged to life, as if affronted that she'd suggest such a thing.

With a trembling hand, she touched his knee. "Then what's stopping you? I have the nanites."

It was as if she'd flipped a switch directly tied to his groin. His hearts pumped rhythmically in his chest, the increased blood flow heightening his awareness of her through every sense. Could he be with her? Dare he? Memories of Aiyana surfaced, but her face was blurred by time, more like a nightmare than a memory. Fresher was the recent memory of Joy's heated kiss in his cabin, her tender mouth beneath his, her soft breasts against his chest.

He scrubbed both hands over his face. "I couldn't bear it if you died. Especially like… that. With me."

"We're likely to die, anyway." Her voice was firmer than he'd expected, and her gaze remained steady. "Let's go out in a blaze of pleasure."

"*Ellam Cua*, woman." But he couldn't deny her. Not her words, not her body, and not her plump and inviting mouth. He reached out and wrapped both hands around her hips, pulling her forward to straddle his lap. "I'm not in control. If I take you, it won't be gentle." His voice sounded like he'd eaten broken glass.

"Let's try." Her fingers threaded through his long hair, forcing his head back ever so slightly. She leaned in and brushed her lips against his like a breath of wind, then her tongue teased the seam of his lips.

He opened his mouth against hers, one hand running up her back to cup the nape of her neck as he savored the kiss. Still, a part of him held back. He murmured against her lips, "I won't be able to stop once I start."

She rocked forward on top of his erection, then back again before sliding one hand down his shoulder and over his hip. Her fingers dipped inside the waistband of his pants, brushing the tip of his throbbing cock. He sucked a breath through his nose, trying with every ounce of strength to control himself. Her hand moved deeper, fingers sliding down his shaft, cupping his balls. He stiffened, unable to breathe as he hardened to the point of pain. His chest burned and his vision hazed. Never had anyone touched him like this.

With a growl, he lifted her off his lap and laid her back on the floor. In the blink of an eye, he'd torn her tunic down the front, exposing the bindings around her breasts. Her nipples poked hard and sharp through the layered fabric. He yanked the binding free, lowering his head to one nipple. The hardened peak against his tongue was ecstasy. A gasp escaped her lips, and she arched into him, nearly toppling him over the edge. He ran his tongue over the silken mound of flesh, nipping and suckling until he reached the other. There, he drew the nipple hard between his lips and she cried out, her fingers digging into his shoulder blades.

His cock throbbed painfully against his pants, but he knew the moment he exposed himself, all would be lost. Instead, he grabbed hold of her waistband, tugging the clothing over her hips to expose her downy sex.

He could have cried with joy. The beauty of her olive skin, the perfect V of curls, the scent of arousal reaching his nostrils was like a taste of heaven. *Ellam Cua*, he'd heard his men speak of tasting a woman. He was going to do more than taste. He was going to devour her. Yanking her legs free, he flung her pants aside before sliding his hands beneath her knees. He drew her legs up and apart, diving into her warm center like a man who'd found an oasis in the desert. She was as savory as honey. He lapped at her folds, her fingers threading into his hair while he stroked his thumbs along the creases of her thighs and feasted.

She moaned, a song that soared through his bloodstream like a drug.

Grabbing hold of the nub of her clit with his lips, he suckled, teasing until she was swollen and throbbing.

Her slickness filled his senses. He wanted to feel every part of her. To make her moan his name as she came around him again and again. Sliding one long finger against her opening, he delved inside.

She bucked against him. "Kashatok!"

His name on her lips was like a prayer. He delved again, and she widened her legs, giving him access to the ridges within her. Her essence coated his hand, filled him with a pleasure he'd only imagined for over fifteen years. Everything was so much better than he remembered. He added a second finger, stroking in and out while he circled her clit with his tongue. He could smell her arousal reaching its peak. Feel her tightening around his fingers. There was nothing in the galaxy better than this, and he'd denied himself too long.

She began to quake and shudder. He slammed his fingers into her again and again, his palm now smacking her sex as he lifted himself on his other hand to peer at her flushed face. She arched against the floor, her bared breasts quivering as she rose to meet his thrusts. His cock surged and jolted, demanding its release. But he couldn't be sure he'd last long enough to finish her, and she deserved pleasure.

A scream erupted from her panting lips, and her core clamped down around his fingers. He didn't stop. He continued driving into her until she sagged, her legs relaxing and her shudders easing. His cock was so hard now, so painful, he doubted he could come if he tried.

She opened her eyes and lifted both hands to reach for him. "I want you."

He needed no more encouragement. With a flick of his fingers, his buckle came loose, his fly was open, and his cock sprang free. Her hands helped ease the waistband down around his hips, the air cool on his exposed flesh. He positioned himself at her entrance, eyes closing as the delicious friction of her heat enveloped the blunt head of his cock.

"*Ellam Cua*," he swore again as he slipped centimeter by centimeter inside her.

She was wet and tight, wrapping him in an embrace he'd never imagined experiencing again. Once he was fully seated inside her, he sighed and remained locked in place for a few moments, reveling in her pulsating heat.

When he opened his eyes, she was looking at him intently, pupils dilated with desire.

She slid her hand beneath his shirt, caressing up his abs until she reached a nipple. She pinched it lightly, sending rockets of pleasure through his nerve endings. Who knew his nipples could be so sensitive?

Slowly, tentatively, he began to move. It was nothing like he remembered from his singular previous experience. Joy was perfect. Joy was pure. Joy was *his*. Her breath washed over him and he took it in, buttocks tightening as he ground against her.

She gasped his name, clinging to him, their gazes locked in what could only be a melding of souls. He increased his speed, pleased when she matched him. Without warning, he became a rutting beast: a primal thing, pounding into her relentlessly, teeth clenched and muscles taut.

He could feel her everywhere, not merely on his cock. Her legs around his hips. Her hands on his torso. Her gaze locked with his. A connection solidified between them, something beyond the physical, beyond the mental, and every stroke hardened the bond.

Even without words, he knew Joy felt it, too. Her eyes were bright with pleasure and love.

Her mouth gaped in a silent scream and she threw her head back, eyes closing as rapture swept through her.

Fear sank its claws into him one last time. "No," he gasped. "Look at me."

He needed to know she was with him. That she wouldn't leave him.

Her lids flew open, and she nodded, still spasming around him. He pumped unrelentingly, driving her through her pleasure. She gripped his shoulders, and he focused his concentration more than he'd ever done before, willing her to rise even higher. To meet him at the precipice. To push him over the edge.

When she crested again, he couldn't stop. He let go, light behind his eyes exploding into pleasure he'd never dreamed possible.

And in that moment he sent his ionic sense into her mind, piercing through the veil that shrouded her thoughts. In that moment, she was his completely.

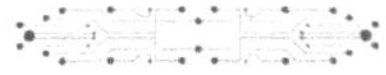

Every synapse in Joy's mind had seemed to alight at once with her orgasm—or was it his? Her senses were flooded with Kashatok, an essence so pure she didn't know where he ended and she began. She could sense his every thought. Every emotion. Right now he was desperate, terrified, full of adrenaline. "Joy, don't leave me. Joy!"

Much like when the wave of data had hit her on the *Kinship*, she was unable to control her body. Her insides still fluttered from the shattering physical release. But she took comfort from the warm arms around her, relaxed into the heated breath against the crook of her neck, breathed deeply of a sweet yet masculine scent that reminded her of rum.

Kashatok.

Slowly, painstakingly, she untangled her thoughts from his, calming her ragged breathing. She opened her eyes, turning her head to meet his gaze. "I'm right here."

He sucked in sharply. *"Ellam Cua,* I thought…"

He shuddered, then his mouth was on hers, his need more emotional than physical. Breaking the kiss, he rested his forehead against hers. "The nanites worked? Praise *Ellam Cua,* you're safe."

She smiled, her camera focusing on the thick fringe of his eyelashes dominating her field of vision. She'd assumed that with the nanites gone, her camera would stop functioning. "I can see."

"That's wonderful." He kissed her again and rolled onto his back, carrying her with him so she rested against his chest. She could hear his dual-beating hearts, strong and sure against her cheek.

"But the nanites should've been destroyed." She peered inside her mind, concentrating on the microcomputers. They no longer floated free about her system. Every single one of them had aligned, coating the myelin sheaths around each nerve cell like armor. The ones on her optic nerves tingled as they transmitted data from her camera, while others had settled into various dormant positions as if awaiting tasks she had yet to assign. Through it all, every one of them thrummed with awareness of the ionic frequency of the man lying beside her. "They're still active."

He stiffened, the hand that had been stroking her back halting sharply. "How can that be?"

She shook her head. She had no idea. Except that in the last moments of climax, something had changed. He'd opened up to her, and she'd glimpsed his essence, the core of his being. And at that moment, she'd become more than herself.

The nanites had changed with her.

He sat up, keeping her on his lap and holding her shoulders to look deeply into her eyes. "*Uminaq,* you need a doctor."

She placed her hands on either side of his bearded face, heart swelling with love for this gruff, protective pirate captain. She wasn't afraid. The machines were a part of her now, as much as her breath or her pulse or her soul. Something she couldn't control yet had become vital to sustaining life. "I don't think they're a danger anymore."

"They're fucking Syndicorp tech. We need to destroy them."

She licked her lips, giving him a mischievous smile, and stroked a finger down his copper-skinned chest toward his navel. "We could try again."

His skin twitched beneath her touch, and from the gap of his open fly, his cock swelled back to life. His pupils dilated as his gaze shifted to her mouth and back to meet her eyes. "I never thought I'd hear a woman say that."

She grinned, wiggling her ass against his legs. Her tunic was ripped to shreds, hanging from her shoulders, so she shrugged out of it. Then she lifted his shirt over his head, exposing his broad chest and muscular shoulders. Damn. Even sitting, the man had washboard abs, his long beard dangling between his pecs.

Pushing him back against the deck, she yanked his pants free. His narrow hips and rock-hard thighs reminded her of the ancient Greek statues Mother'd forced her to study after Joy'd professed a desire to be an artist. While the statues had been drool-worthy, Mother's drive for perfection had nipped Joy's love of art in the bud.

Now she regained her appreciation, running her palms up Kashatok's naked legs, pausing where his groin rose into a massive erection unlike any she'd ever seen on a Greek statue. Her pussy tightened, its soreness reminding her of the Earth-shattering orgasms she'd just experienced. Despite the ache in her core, she wanted another one.

She lifted a leg and straddled him, continuing to smooth her palms up his chest to his shoulders.

He grabbed her hips and pulled her down, trapping his erection between them. She tilted her hips, and he pulled her tighter, grinding his length against her clit. A shudder raced through her, and she lifted her chin in an involuntary moan of pleasure.

Sitting up again, he slipped his broad hands around to cup her ass, fingertips feathering the outer edges of her sex. She was slippery, throbbing, heated. Leaning in, she breathed in his masculine scent. He met her move, biting softly at her bottom lip before claiming her in a kiss that made her nipples harden and her nanites fire with anticipation. Each stroke of his tongue within her mouth built the fire within her higher and hotter, until she was rocking against him, her lower lips embracing his length in tantalizing strokes.

Lifting her as if she weighed nothing, he settled her back down, spearing her with his cock. She gasped as his thick head pulsed deep inside her. Holy hell, she was going to come again, and they'd barely started. Her hips twitched, needing to move, but he ground her firmly against him, his mouth devouring hers. Whatever he was doing was building a pressure deep within her like she'd never experienced, as if his cock was growing in size, stretching her to the fullest.

When he finally relaxed his hold, allowing a breath of space between them, the delightful friction sent micro-orgasms shuddering through her.

Then he began to undulate his hips beneath her, rocking side to side. "Kashatok," she gasped, meeting his rhythm, eyes locked on his.

He lay back, bringing her with him. The shift deepened his penetration, hitting a spot just below her navel that made her shiver. She rocked her hips, building to a frenzy while bracing herself with both hands against his rock-hard chest.

He slid a hand between them, thumb circling her clit.

Jolts of pleasure fired through her, igniting her nanites to new levels of awareness, additional levels of pleasure. She settled into a rhythm that drowned out all else, riding him until it felt as if every synapse would explode.

"Joy," he grunted, his hands running up her sides to cup her breasts. He pinched her nipples ever so lightly, but the added sensation sent fire through her bloodstream. Every muscle in her body convulsed with her orgasm. His release took him at the same moment, filling her with his heat and leaving her breathless.

CHAPTER FIFTEEN

Hours later, Kashatok roused as Joy's warmth left him, and she moved to the lavatory. Much as he reveled in watching everything she did, he rolled over, cradling his head on his wadded-up shirt. The elated contentment pulsing through him felt as if his body was trying to catch up on fifteen years of deprivation. It almost masked the hopelessness of the situation they were in.

Joy returned, shivering in the chill of the pod's struggling life support system. How long did they have before the energy cells were depleted? He pulled his shirt from beneath his head. "Here, put this on."

The hem fell almost to her knees. His cock stirred yet again. He couldn't get enough of her. "I like you in my clothes."

She pursed her lips, fighting back a smile. "Are you warm enough?"

"Never better." He held an arm up, inviting her to snuggle against him.

He wrapped both arms around her, spooning against her while he breathed deeply against her hair. It felt as if he might wake up from a dream at any moment.

She kissed his forearm. "I'm sorry I got you into this."

He could honestly say that if he died now, he'd die content. But the thought of Joy's life being extinguished was nearly unbearable. "It's not your fault. I think you merely provided Aleknagik with an excuse to do something he's wanted to do for years. Finding out you were Mulholland-Aird's daughter was just something he capitalized on to rally the crew against me."

Her hands clenched into fists. "My damn mother."

His arms tightened. He'd told her he believed she wasn't Syndicorp, but how could she not be? "So… how *is* the CEO's daughter not with the corp'?"

Joy sighed, her breath tickling his arm before she sat up to face him. She drew her knees inside the shirt and hugged them against her. "Mother and I have never seen eye-to-eye. She wanted me to follow in her footsteps, yet I was never pretty enough, charismatic enough, or even worse, *dedicated* enough in her opinion. The entire reason I became a reporter was because I thought if I made anchor, she'd have to respect that. She watches the news all the time. She knows more about what's going on in the finofan bureaucracy than she does about her own family. She didn't even realize I was gone until I called her."

His stomach did a flip-flop. "You called her?"

Joy blanched, then nodded. "Like I said, this is all my fault."

Kashatok sat up to face her. "So, you *were* reporting to her?"

"No!" Joy's eyes widened, and he felt her blood pressure spike through their lingering ionic connection. "I just… after you said you were a *carayak*, I couldn't stomach someone else… destroying the nanites, so I hacked into the *Hardship's* comm and called Mother, thinking she would know where to send me for help."

Any growing rancor he felt about her subsided. She hadn't wanted anyone but him. It was one thing to dangle love before him and snatch it away once. But twice? *Ellam Cua* couldn't be that cruel. "Any chance your mother's sending help now?"

Joy shook her head. "I don't think she even knows which quadrant I'm in. I cut the connection as soon as she suggested sending troopers. And the emergency beacon is only sending a generic long-range transmission. She has no way to know I'm on board."

He waved a hand at the star-studded void outside the small view screen. "For all we know, there's a space station just out of sensor range."

Chewing her lip, Joy stared at the view screen. "We need to boost our signal." She scooted forward and popped open the compartment below the control panel. "If I up the amperage and integrate the sensors to latch onto any nearby signals, we may be able to increase our range." She paused and looked over her shoulder at him. "But it will use up all our extra juice. Our life support will be reduced by days. What if no one hears us? Or they do, but can't reach us in time?"

For a long moment he looked at her, the woman he loved. The future he'd never have. Their chance of surviving was already slim to nothing. Was there a wrong choice in this situation? "I think we should try."

She nodded and pointed at the compartment holding the pod's tools. "Hand me the smallest spanner you can find."

After several hours of tinkering, Joy wiped her hands on the rags of her shirt and disengaged the pod's gravity to save energy. "We're broadcasting." Her short hair made a halo around her head as she floated free of the cabin floor. "I'd say we have less than half a day of power using these levels."

Kashatok pulled her close, wrapping both arms around her middle and spinning lazily in the center of the cabin. "I'm not ready for this to end."

"I know. Me either." She grabbed his beard, tugging gently to bring his mouth down to hers. The kiss she gave him lingered long and slow, heating his blood with a soft tenderness they'd not indulged in previously. Breaking the kiss, she looked deeply into his eyes. "Do you believe in an afterlife?"

Although he knew she could only see him through her camera, she saw the real him. She knew his darkest secret and didn't shy away. The mate bond—something he'd given up ever hoping could be his—had created a tangible thread between them. "*Ellam Cua* promises when we find our mates, the bond will be true and after death, we'll be united to experience new dimensions, new purpose."

"That's a lot to hope for." She let out a trembling laugh. "Now that you're not a *carayak*, you can have your pick of women with nanites. Sure you don't want to trade me in for a better model if we make the next port?"

If he hadn't been so attuned to her, he might've mistaken her words for a brush off. "You're the most beautiful woman in the universe, Joy. My mate. My heart. My everything."

Her entire body heated within his embrace, her face lighting with a smile. "I love you, too."

He ran one hand up her back and threaded his fingers through her short hair, memorizing her face, enjoying her closeness for what might be the last time. "This has been the happiest time in my entire life."

"Mine, too." Joy's eyes widened abruptly, her gaze drilling past him toward the view screen. "Holy hell, Kashatok, there's a ship!"

Kashatok twisted, looking out the port. His breath caught at the oblong module covered in Syndicorp markings. "Troopers."

Pawing her way through the air toward the viewport, Joy pressed her face next to his. "We're saved!"

Gritting his teeth, he nodded. He was a wanted man, sure to be executed at the next port—if not immediately. Syndicorp gave no quarter to pirates.

As if sensing his concern, she asked, "What's wrong?"

"Nothing, my love." He ran his knuckles along the side of her face. "You're saved, and that's all that matters."

"Oh, shit." Her face paled. "You're a pirate."

He nodded, giving her a resigned smile. "I always assumed I'd die in a firefight, not under a Syndicorp executioner's needle."

"That's not going to happen. You saved me. My mother has to pardon you." She elbowed him aside and switched on the comm. "Trooper vessel, this is Joy Mulholland-Aird on board the escape pod. Do you copy?"

Long moments passed with no answer. Outside the view screen, the trooper ship drifted against its background of stars, as if oblivious to their presence.

"Is it possible they don't know we're here?" she asked.

"Try another channel."

She cycled through the three distress channels, each with no response. Pulling herself downward to the base of the console, she traced the exposed wiring beneath the control panel. "Everything looks fine here." She lifted her head and looked out the view screen again. "Maybe they're having trouble with their sensors? We're hardly bigger than space dust in this pod. We might be out of visible range."

He nodded slowly. Something wasn't right. Trooper protocol was to check for survivors. "I think we should move in. Get close enough for them to get a visual."

"We don't have enough power for thrusters."

"Yes, we do. It just reduces our life support from hours to minutes." He hated to put them in further jeopardy, but there was the possibility the other ship could move on at any moment. "We have to do something." He hooked the toes of his boots at the base of the console and engaged the thrusters to swing the pod toward the troopers.

At the edge of the view screen, another ship appeared. Kashatok's heart caught in his throat. The *Hardship*. Captain Qaiyaan had come for them after all. *Come for Joy*. The other pirate owed nothing to Kashatok.

Purple bolts of light flashed over the trooper's hull. "God, is that the *Hardship*?" Joy asked. "They're firing at each other!"

The familiar shape of Captain Qaiyaan's ship dodged around the other vessel, evading its blasters while pummeling the troopers with its smaller gunfire. A stray blaster bolt bathed the view screen in a florescent glow.

"*Uminaq!*" Kashatok reached for the controls to guide them away from the fight.

Every light on the console flickered and went out. Then the low hum of the air scrubbers went silent. Using the thrusters had killed the last of the power reserves. Kashatok bellowed, "No!"

Bursts of light from the battle outside lit Joy's terrified face with deeply cut shadows. He could feel her trembling and pulled her into his arms. "We're heading straight into the line of fire."

She pressed her cheek against his chest. "Are we close enough to use your cochlear implant to call out?"

The implant had a short range, but it was worth a shot. He tapped below his ear. "This is Kashatok aboard the escape pod. Does anyone copy?"

"We read you, Captain!" Qaiyaan's voice came back immediately. "What the hell do you think you're doing? Reverse thrusters, now!"

Kashatok's hearts thumped as if they were knocking together. "Thrusters are down! Stop firing! Tell the troopers Joy's on board."

"Those aren't troopers, Captain."

Kashatok gripped Joy tighter. "Who are they?"

Tovik's voice cut in. "Kashatok, you have to evacuate the pod!"

"I told you, Joy's with me," Kashatok nearly shouted. "We have no vacuum suits."

"You'll only have to hold your shield around both of you for a few minutes. Push off the pod perpendicular to us with every bit of ionic power you can spare. We'll keep Aleknagik occupied and hopefully he won't notice. Then we can give him the pod while we sweep by and pick you up."

The pod shuddered as a blast passed close by. "I don't understand. How is Aleknagik shooting at us?"

"He commandeered the fucking trooper ship!" Qaiyaan said. "Now either evacuate or prepare to be blown to cosmic dust."

"We can do this, Kashatok," Tovik said. "I won't let you two die."

Kashatok believed the kid. Seemed to be a habit of his to believe people lately. He took a breath and pushed Joy off his chest. "They want us to evacuate."

"How?" The look on her face was almost comical in the strobing purple light.

"My ionic shielding. Like we did when we jumped off the slave ship."

She swallowed loud enough for him to hear. "Are we near enough to do that?"

"No. But Tovik says he has a plan."

"Much as I like Tovik, jumping into space without a suit and nowhere to land sounds like the stupidest plan ever."

A crazed chuckle rumbled through him. He felt absolutely insane right now. "They want us to space-lock ourselves."

She took a deep breath. "I trust you. Just tell me what to do."

They might die out there, but they were definitely on course to die if they stayed here. He turned around. "Hop on my back."

She wrapped her legs around his hips and gripped his shoulders.

He wrapped his hands beneath her knees to hold her against him. "Take a bunch of quick breaths, like you're hyperventilating."

He followed his own advice, saturating his bloodstream with oxygen before raising his shield.

"Popping the air seal now," he said into his implant.

The small cabin evacuated its atmosphere like a sigh. Against the velvet blackness, the two ships looked like toys in the distance.

Kashatok bent his knees and jumped.

He probably should've put more force behind his leap, but he wanted to be sure he reserved enough strength to maintain his shielding. Far out to his left, the troopers and the *Hardship* seemed evenly matched, purple pulses of light strafing the blackness between them. Both vessels wove around each other in evasive maneuvers. How could Qaiyaan possibly break away before Kashatok ran out of energy for his shield? Locking his forearms more firmly beneath Joy's knees, he prayed to *Ellam Cua* for a miracle.

Joy clung to Kashatok's back, unsure if she needed to hold her breath. Just to be safe, she did. Far off to her left, the two vessels continued exchanging fire. The vastness of space surrounding them felt like a monster's jaws, ready to swallow them at any moment. She'd hoped Kashatok's super-power included some kind of propulsion, but he only drifted in the direction he'd jumped, his arms clamped around her knees.

Then the *Hardship* suddenly spun on its axis and darted straight for them. A bolt from the trooper ship's long-range cannon whizzed past, too close for Joy's comfort. A sip of air escaped her lips, and she clamped her mouth closed to contain what she had left in her lungs.

Then a crushing hand seemed to grab hold of her, freezing every limb in position. *The tractor beam? Oh, God.* It was designed to move metallic structures like ship hulls, not living flesh. She hoped their young engineer knew what he was doing.

The *Hardship* seemed to double in size. Then double again. Without warning, the tractor beam cut off, releasing the bone-crushing pressure. The ship continued to rush toward them, the open maw of the cargo hold several ship-lengths away. Whoever was piloting the ship had better have a damn steady hand, or she and Kashatok would end up as nothing but smears against the hull.

She pressed her cheek to the side of Kashatok's neck, wishing she could take one last breath, smell him one last time. The hatch was nearly within reach now, the opening hazed by a sparkling atmospheric force-shield.

Three meters.

Two.

Kashatok ducked, his top-knot almost brushing the bay's door frame as they shot into the lit interior and slammed into a cargo net strung inside the hold. Joy's breath exploded in a giant rush, her hold on Kashatok broken. Like a slow-motion rubber band, the netting stretched…

The rebound flung her back in the direction they'd come from. Terror that she might be ejected through the open door seized her; instead, she crashed into the opposite wall of the cargo bay.

The impact felt like it had bruised every inch of her body. Her camera winked out. Barely conscious, she felt someone lift her.

"They're in," Mek said.

Next thing she knew, she was lying on a mattress. Hands pressed diodes to her temples. A familiar furry body brushed against her cheek, settling at the crook of her neck and shoulder.

"Jhikik?" she slurred, unable to open her eyes.

The netorpok purred softly, nuzzling his head beneath her ear. Where was Kashatok? Before she could rally the strength to open her eyes, the familiar vertigo of burn twisted her inside out. Nausea rose and fell, her muscles quivered, every vein in her body seemed to be filled with lava. After long, excruciating minutes, the sensation ended.

She let out a sigh. Her body throbbed from hitting the cargo wall, but compared to the last couple of burns, her head didn't feel so bad. Even the nanites had remained sane. In fact, they were silent as the grave. Curious, she commanded, *Camera.*

Light stabbed into her brain and she squeezed her eyes shut, adjusting her filters before trying again. Next to her ear, Jhikik clacked his teeth.

Kashatok's voice came from somewhere near her feet. "How is she? I need to see her."

She lifted her head, noting the familiar surroundings of the *Hardship's* med bay. Kashatok leaned on the door frame, looking haggard as hell, but alive. *Thank God.* She dropped her head back against the pillow. "I'm okay. A little beat up, but alive." She extended a hand toward him. "How're you?"

He moved up the side of the cot, the furious lines of his face softening. Behind him at the computer, Mek watched them with his arms crossed.

Kashatok wove his fingers between hers. "I can't believe that worked."

"Me either." Her heart felt so full, it hurt almost as much as her bruised body.

Jhikik scurried over their connected hands, perching on Kashatok's shoulder. A contented purr filled the room.

"Good to see you, too." Kashatok rubbed the netorpok beneath the chin.

Joy sighed. "Do you know what's going on?"

"Maybe *you* can tell *us*, Ms. Mulholland-Aird." Noatak's voice cut through the room like a laser.

Her heart leaped into her throat. *They're going to kill me.* But they wouldn't go through the effort of rescuing her only to kill her, would they? Not before they harvested the nanites.

Kashatok widened his stance, standing between her and Noatak. "Back off."

Tovik tore around the corner into the med bay, his face alight. "*Anaq,* you guys! That was *awesome!*"

"Not now, Tovik," Noatak warned without taking his gaze off Joy.

Mek pointed to Joy and Kashatok's joined hands. "They've mated."

Heat crept over Joy's face while Kashatok strengthened his grip on her hand. "Yes."

Noatak's face darkened. "So the nanites are gone?"

"Oh, crap," Tovik said. "Qaiyaan's going to be pissed."

Mek picked up a syringe. "Perhaps I can still learn something from her blood."

Even without ionic senses of her own, Joy felt Kashatok's power expand. He let go of her hand and snatched the syringe from Mek's grip. "No one touches her."

Joy pushed the diodes away from her head and sat up painfully. "Kashatok, it's okay. Let him take a sample." She held her arm out to Mek. "I know you said the mating frequency would destroy the nanites, but they're not gone."

Mek's gaze sharpened. "Interesting. Let's take a look."

She looked away while he pressed the sample gun against her arm.

Qaiyaan rounded the corner and stopped in the doorway. "Mek, Lisa needs your attention before we can jump again." He stiffened, eyes narrowing as he looked at the gathered men. "What's wrong?"

"She's mated," Noatak clipped out.

"But I still have the nanites," Joy added, willing herself not to turn away from Qaiyaan's furious look.

"I'll know in a moment," Mek said, plugging her blood sample into his diagnostic machine. Joy's camera jounced in time with her heartbeat while she waited. After a moment, Mek shook his head, turning back to face the room. "There are no nanites in her bloodstream."

"What?" Joy could barely form words. She didn't want to think of what might happen to her if she didn't have the nanites to bargain with. "There has to be. My camera's working."

Face doubtful, Mek pulled a scanner from the cupboard. "Most likely, your optic nerve has simply returned to normal. Let me take a reading of your synaptic system."

Passing the scanner slowly over her scalp, he made a surprised noise and repeated the motion. Setting the scanner aside, he scratched his cheek. "I don't know how, but she still has them. It appears the nanites have secured themselves to her nervous system."

The entire room seemed to breathe a sigh of relief. Joy's sigh was loudest of all. "So that's good, right? We didn't kill them. Why aren't they showing up in my blood?"

Mek shook his head. "They're no longer free floating."

"What does that mean?" Kashatok grumbled.

"I can't harvest her," Mek said. "At least not the way I'd imagined."

The word harvest had Joy's blood racing, and she was grateful when Kashatok spoke with caveman-like protectiveness. "You're not harvesting my mate."

"Bad choice of words." Mek held up a placating hand. "I meant to say gather excess nanites."

Kashatok's fists knotted at his sides. "Whatever she has or doesn't have, she's my mate. I won't let any of you hurt her."

"Me either." Tovik glared at Noatak.

"She's Syndicorp, you fools." Noatak took a step forward. "Probably in league with Aleknagik this entire time."

Jhikik clicked his teeth at the advancing crewman.

Joy's jaw dropped. "Aleknagik's with Syndicorp?"

"No, fucking way," Kashatok shook his head. "He may've taken me by surprise with the mutiny, but if there's one thing Aleknagik is not, it's Syndicorp. He's just a bastard who subverted my crew and stole my ship. Where the hell is my ship, anyway?"

"We left it behind to rescue you," Qaiyaan said. "Are you sure he's not with the corp'?"

"Positive."

Qaiyaan shook his head, brow furrowed. "Aleknagik probably went straight back to where we left the *Kinship*. He'll be waiting, and we're no match for those trooper guns."

"Suicide mission," Noatak added.

Chapter Sixteen

S*uicide mission*, Kashatok thought, remembering Chignik's helpless confession to him in the brig. "Who's left on the *Kinship*?"

"Not sure. We didn't stick around for roll call," Qaiyaan said.

Tovik added, "Aleknagik took two guys with him."

Joy's hand slipped into his. "I'm worried about Gassy."

Kashatok nodded, his gaze locked with Qaiyaan's. "They're my *iluq*," he said softly. "I owe them my help." For the first time in over fifteen years, he realized he wanted that sense of brotherhood.

"I understand." Qaiyaan crossed his arms. "But if we let the nanites be destroyed, that's the end of any hope for future mates."

"If we don't make a point of protecting our fellow denaidans, we have no reason for mates," Kashatok pointed out. "Losing the men on the *Kinship* would be a major loss when there are so few of us left."

A pained look crossed Qaiyaan's face. He rubbed his forehead. "One impossible situation after another. First, my mate is wanted by the cartel. Now your mate is being tracked by Syndicorp. *Anaq,* we have terrible taste in women, Kashatok."

The men chuckled, and even Kashatok had to smile. "I'm just grateful to have found a mate at all."

Joy's brows furrowed. "But if Aleknagik's not with Syndicorp, how'd he end up in control of the trooper ship?"

Qaiyaan smirked. "We're pirates. It's what we do."

Kashatok squeezed her knee. "Superpowers, remember? We surprise and board ships that way all the time."

"Oh. Right." Joy groaned and pushed herself off the cot. "Tovik, is the piggyback harness still in place on the *Kinship?*"

"Yeah. Why?"

"If we catch Aleknagik between our two ships while

engaging the piggyback, wouldn't it blow out his power coils?"

Tovik let out a low whistle. "Theoretically, yes. But that last piggyback knocked us apart. We'd need them to recalibrate."

"How do we do that when they're being guarded?" Qaiyaan stroked his beard.

"I could talk them through it if we were in comm range," Tovik said.

Noatak shook his head. "Aleknagik knows all our comm channels. He will be monitoring them."

"I have the nanites," Joy said. "I can connect straight into the *Kinship's* comm and walk them through the calibration without Aleknagik being any the wiser. Although…" She bit her bottom lip. "We'll need to be fairly close to do that."

"Our shields are no match for trooper cannons," Qaiyaan said.

"Let me handle the controls," Kashatok said. "I've piloted through worse."

Qaiyaan raised his brows. "I know your piloting is legendary, but are you sure?"

Imagining blowing Aleknagik to space dust, Kashatok grinned. "Just show me to the cockpit."

He was going to get his damn ship back if it killed him.

The makeshift nav-grav seat Tovik had rigged in engineering barely held Joy steady as the *Hardship* changed trajectories again. With her camera deactivated so she could use the nanites for the comm, blindness had her panicking every time the ship shuddered under impact.

"Whoa, that was a close one," Tovik reported from somewhere in engineering as he worked on calibrating the *Hardship's* drive. "How're things going over on the *Kinship?*"

Still reeling from post-burn nausea, Joy'd contacted Ekwok on the *Kinship's* bridge. Gassy was still down, however, and none of the crew knew much about engineering. Cooper and Chignik had been taking the instructions she was relaying on how to adjust the harness, but were now debating each other on the other end of the comm.

"Listen up," Joy strengthened the nanites' signal, needing to sound authoritative before she lost them all together.

"Stop arguing and tighten the hex bolt another quarter turn, then send me the numbers."

Joy's heart raced as she waited for the data. How long could Kashatok evade Aleknagik's guns yet remain close enough to the *Kinship* for her to keep contact? And that wasn't even the hard part; once the harness was aligned, they had to maneuver Aleknagik's ship between the other two ships and hit the burn drive.

Data streamed over the comm, and she immediately relayed the information to Tovik's console. "Please tell me they've got it close enough."

Chignik's transmission through the nanites was asking the same thing. Tovik mumbled, "Maybe if I make an adjustment to our flux membrane…"

The ship jerked, lifting her from the seat before the chair's harness caught her and slammed her back against the padding. Tovik grunted.

The internal comm exploded with Noatak's voice. "Direct hit! Shields at eighteen percent. Engineering, you'd better have things ready soon."

No answer from Tovik.

"Tovik?" she asked. *Damn this blindness.* "You okay?"

His strained voice answered her. "Go ahead and let the *Kinship* know they're good." He cleared his throat. "Captain, we're ready to line them up."

"Chignik, Cooper, that did it," Joy sent. "Tovik says to hold on tight. Things may get rough over there."

She gripped the arms of the nav-grav chair and hoped her plan wasn't about to blow them all up.

Kashatok clenched his sweaty hands over the yoke, guiding the Kinship through evasive maneuvers while Noatak manned the co-pilot seat.

The tiny bridge could barely hold two men, and Qaiyaan had given up his seat to operate the ship's gun turret. Never would Kashatok have imagined having respect for a man who willingly relinquished his ship, but Captain Qaiyaan had managed to maintain his regard. He was a damn good shot with that gun, as well, taking down one of the trooper vessel's short-range lasers despite Kashatok's crazy flying.

"Captain, we're ready to line them up," Tovik sent over the ship's internal comm.

Kashatok was ready. He spun the ship on its axis, heading straight for the troopers. The smaller *Hardship* had great maneuverability, but he'd gauged that he'd need to get within meters of the trooper vessel to be in range of the *Kinship's* harness field.

Kashatok held the yoke steady, staring down the barrels of three lasers. His gaze flickered between the deadly menace and the range sensor on his dash. "Full shields to the forward panels."

Purple strobes of light hit the Hardship face-on and rendered the view screen temporarily useless.

Anaq.

Relying on sensors alone, Kashatok held his course.

Noatak's voice cracked from the co-pilot seat. "Forward shields holding at fifteen percent."

The wail of proximity alarms filled the cabin.

Kashatok's hands remained steady, even though his mind was screaming at him to pull up.

Two more heartbeats.

Now. Praying to *Ellam Cua,* Kashatok hit the burn drive and pulled up on the yoke.

The inertial force flattened him into the seat and made it hard to breathe. The familiar nausea of the burn drive swelled over him, but that feeling of being sucked through a straw never came. He squinted at his sensors and twisted the yoke to bring the ship back around.

Through the view screen, the *Kinship* floated as before, the familiar pattern of stars the only backdrop.

Aleknagik's ship was gone.

"Where'd they go?" Noatak asked, fingertips flying over the sensor controls.

Kashatok's insides contracted. That had been too easy. "Look for debris."

He called up the sensor readings on his own panel, backtracking through the data to find the precise moment he'd hit the burn drive.

Qaiyaan poked his head inside the cockpit. "What the hell just happened?"

"Trying to figure that out, Captain," Noatak said without looking up.

"I'm going to check on Lisa. She's been ill, enduring so many burns in a row."

Kashatok sucked in a breath and rose from his seat. Joy probably felt the same way, and he'd been focused on Aleknagik. He tapped the comm to engineering. "How's Joy?"

"I'm okay," her voice came from behind Qaiyaan. The big captain stepped aside and let her move into his spot. "Tovik's got a nasty bump, though."

Relieved as he was to see her well, Kashatok's throat tightened. "The bastard got away."

"What do you mean?" Her eyebrows drew together.

He slumped back down into the pilot's chair. She moved into the cramped space to stand behind him. He pointed to the burn data on his console. "I need more time to go over the details. We're in the same location, but there was a frequency dilation."

"*Anaq*," Noatak punched more buttons next to him. "He burned out of here?"

"Wherever he ended up, he's nothing more than flotsam now." Joy leaned over Kashatok's shoulder for a closer look at the screen. "The energy certainly arced out his power coils."

Kashatok reached up and cupped her other cheek. "I have what matters most. You're safe."

"And you can have your ship back." She squeezed his shoulders and pressed her cheek against his.

Kashatok nodded, still staring at the *Kinship.*

He hoped Aleknagik had ended up in the middle of a star.

239

Kashatok strode across the boarding tube onto the *Kinship*. Waiting on the other side, Ekwok and Cooper pumped their fists while Chignik strode forward and clapped Kashatok on one shoulder. "You're one hell of a pilot, Captain." Nodding to Joy, who remained a little behind Kashatok, he smiled. "Good job talking us through those calibrations, too."

Kashatok sensed her stiffness ease, but she remained near the boarding tube, which Kashatok appreciated. She'd insisted on coming along and having his back, and Jhikik had insisted on coming with her, curled at the crook of her neck. Next to Joy, Qaiyaan stood with his hands near the pistols on his belt.

Cooper smoothed a big palm over his bald, tattooed head. "We want to say we're real sorry things went like they did, Captain. Aleknagik played us all against each other."

"Chignik was the only one he had nothing on," Ekwok added.

Kashatok glanced over the three men, his heart still hard over the mutiny. "You the only three left on board?"

"Gassy's in the med bay. We put Manopup and Moore in the brig," Chignik said. "They were still woozy from burn when Aleknagik jumped ship or they'd've gone, too."

"They'd been whispering mutiny for a long time." Cooper ducked his head. "I thought it was just talk."

The muscles in Kashatok's jaw tightened as he considered what he was going to do to the men in his brig. Space-locking seemed too kind.

"Gassy's been asking for you," Ekwok volunteered.

Joy stepped forward. "Is he okay?"

"I think so," Ekwok said. "But Doc's gone with Aleknagik, so I can't say for sure."

Their betrayal hurt, but at least they'd surrendered his ship back to him. He cleared his throat. "Qaiyaan," he turned to address his fellow captain, "may we borrow your doctor?"

"I'll send him over." Qaiyaan nodded and headed back to his own ship.

Kashatok extended a hand to Joy. "Let's go check on Gassy."

In the med bay, Gassy was propped against some pillows. He looked just as hellacious as before, but at least he was sitting up instead of lying there like a dying fish. Kashatok stopped just inside the med bay, noting the sterility shield over the bed was down. "You're breathing normal air again. How're you feeling, old man?"

"Couldn't take another breath inside that shield. I hear I better get my ass up and moving soon 'cause this little lady's after my job," he said with a twinkle in his eye.

Joy moved forward and took the old man's hand. "I could never replace you. You still have a lot to teach me."

"Don't worry, you're not getting rid of me quite yet," Gassy said.

Kashatok approached the bedside until his shoulder touched Joy's, loving the subtle way she leaned into him. "Qaiyaan's doc will be over soon to check you out."

"If anyone can make you well, Mek can," Joy added.

"Take it you've had reason to be in his med bay?" Gassy's astute gaze swept across their connected shoulders.

Joy flushed a delightful pink.

Kashatok couldn't help the grin that felt like it might crack his face in two. He lifted his arm to pull Joy firmly against him, resting his chin atop her head. Gassy'd always told him he should question the assumption he was a *carayak*. Never had Kashatok been so grateful to admit he'd been wrong. "You were right all along."

"'Course I was." Gassy's blistered face sobered. "Just remember, the rest of us aren't as lucky as you are."

Kashatok removed his chin from Joy's head, but kept his arm around her. He wasn't used to being one of the lucky ones. "We're going to help change that."

Joy nodded. "We're going to help Qaiyaan locate Syndicorp's secret lab."

Gassy tilted his head. "That's well and good. But you have other things to consider first."

It wasn't like Gassy to be negative. Frowning, Kashatok asked, "What do you mean?"

The old man shook his grizzled head. "With Aleknagik gone, you're going to need more crew. And you don't exactly have the best reputation in the galaxy."

Kashatok cringed, remembering how difficult it'd been to hire a shuttle mechanic. What would his reputation be like after losing three more crewmen, including his first mate? Looking at Joy, he realized things didn't need to be difficult; she was as charming as he was gruff. He grinned at her. "I have a new first mate who can do the interviewing for me."

Joy sucked in a breath, twisting to look up at him. "Me?"

"Sure," he said. "There's no one I trust more."

"What about Gassy?"

"Leave me out of this," Gassy said. "I'm old and one of these days I'll have enough money to retire in a cushy flat at some exotic port."

She scrunched her nose and seemed to consider. "Will your men even listen to me?"

The sound of a throat clearing behind him made him turn. Chignik stood in the doorway, the rest of the crew in the hallway at his back. "You busted our captain out of the brig, made a daring escape, then came back for more. I'd say you earned it."

The others nodded. Pride in Joy made Kashatok stand a little straighter.

Gassy coughed. "That settles it then. Now get out and let an old man get some rest, would you?"

Giving Joy's shoulders one last squeeze, Kashatok ushered her out the door. It was time to get his ship up and running.

Epilogue

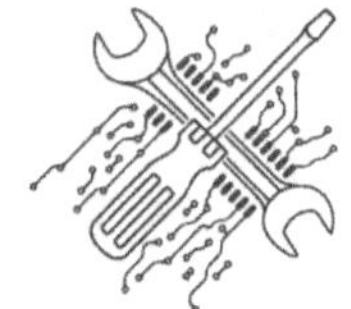

Joy stared out Kashatok's cabin window on the *Kinship,* the faint outline of her reflection in the glass overlaying the jutting buttresses of the space station outside. She wore one of his billowy shirts, enveloping herself in his ginger-cinnamon scent. How many times had they made love since she'd become the *Kinship's* first mate? She felt like she'd finally found a place where she belonged, doing exactly what she was meant to do. Never in her life had she imagined feeling so complete.

As if to reflect her own happiness back at her, the leaves of the naujiar plant rustled, contented cheeps echoing among the foliage. Kashatok had given Jhikik open access to the plant to keep him occupied after Joy pointed out how fascinated the netorpok seemed to be by their intimate activities. And there'd been a lot of activity. She turned to face where he still lounged on the rumpled bed, one deliciously sculpted leg outside the sheets while he read his polycom.

But she needed to stay focused on their immediate problem. Qaiyaan'd towed them to the port, and she'd installed the new flux inverter, but they had yet to fill the empty crew positions. Kashatok's reputation was proving hard to overcome. She climbed onto the corner of the mattress and knelt, settling back against her heels. "People like stories about pirates."

"As villains." Kashatok's voice rumbled sexily as he lowered the polycom to his lap. She loved how he seemed to follow her train of thought, no matter how out of the blue her comments might be.

"What if we provided a different angle to the story?" She tapped her left temple. "Say… an exposé about pirate freedom fighters?"

He laughed, a sound she loved more and more the freer he became with his joy. He lunged forward and pulled her against him, flopping to his back with her resting on his hard abs. "Are you suggesting we start a revolution?"

She chewed her lip. She'd been thinking about it a lot, actually. After learning what Syndicorp had done, what her mother had done—not only killing off an entire race but covering it up—she'd become determined to blow the lid off the entire thing. "I'm suggesting we put out a call to action. I'm still on staff at RealTime News. I can spin the exposé into a thinly veiled advertisement to hire crew and find suitable candidates for denaidan mates."

His big hands stopped massaging her naked rump. "Advertise for mates?"

"There's no reason new crew members can't be female, is there? And if they find a love interest while they're here, even better." She pushed up, straddling his hips. "Let's put a call out to men and women who want to overcome the tyranny that's taken over every planet in the galaxy."

"An adventure in the swashbuckling world of black market trading and deep-space piracy?" His upturned mouth looked completely kissable as he teased her with the line from her original recording.

"I should've never shared that video with you." She smacked his chest and lifted a knee half-heartedly as if to dismount.

He grabbed her hips, securing her in place over the line of his growing erection, separated by only the thin layer of the sheet between them. "Ah, but there's only one rule on board my ship."

She narrowed her eyes. "Rule? You're not still trying to ban women, are you? Because as your first mate—"

"More of a request than a rule." He ran both hands up beneath the loose shirt to cup her breasts. "I want you to share everything with me."

His thumbs found her nipples and teased them to sensitive nubs. Her back arched involuntarily. For a moment, she simply reveled in the way he played her body. There was no need for words when he already knew her so well. She recalled something Lisa had told her over lunch yesterday. "Lisa said she and Qaiyaan can hear each other's thoughts. Do you think we'll ever be that close?"

His bottomless dark eyes drank her in. "Whether or not we ever can, you're my first mate, my only mate. There is no future without you."

She placed a hand against his chest, finding the twin thump of his hearts. Hearts that beat only for her. Being loved unconditionally was more beautiful than she'd ever imagined.

Leaning forward, she pressed her forehead against his, taking satisfaction that she had beaten all the odds to gain his love. "I will always love you," she vowed. "You are my mate."

One of his hands slid up to the back of her neck, pulling her into a kiss. His tongue teased open her mouth, swirling and stroking and building a heat within her while his rock-hard length grew more insistent between her legs. His other hand continued massaging her breast and nipple, moving to her ribs, down to her hip, and back up again in a teasing caress that made her skin tremble and twitch until the heat between them became a raging inferno.

"I need to be in you," he said.

"Yes," she breathed out, lifting herself so he could pull the thin sheet aside. She poised her opening over the blunt head of his cock. Then slowly, deliberately, she lowered herself against him, eyes locked with his in a connection so intimate, it wouldn't have mattered if they were touching or not. The delicious friction of his length entering her ran clear up her spine.

For long moments, she stayed locked in place, her gaze trapped by his. Reaching forward, she brushed her fingers against his cheek, then trailed them down the length of his beard.

Slowly, subtly, she began to move, rocking and lifting her hips at just the right angle to send flutters of ecstasy throughout her entire body.

He was right there with her, hips thrusting upward. His speed increased to match hers, ratcheting up her pleasure.

She was aware of him everywhere. Not just deep in her inner wetness, but pressed between her thighs, under her fingertips, sharing her air. His hands guided her hips, but it was as if he knew her every desire, anticipated every move before she even knew herself.

His eyes on her were bright with pleasure and love. "You're so amazing."

The first wave of pleasure hit her, shuddering through her body and nearly paralyzing her. But Kashatok didn't stop. He continued pumping upward unrelentingly, holding her hips and taking her past the first crest and onto another. Her mouth opened in a silent scream. She leaned forward and gripped his shoulders, her entire body throbbing with the connection. It wasn't like a psychic connection, but one of emotion. A bond solidifying between them like nothing she'd ever imagined possible.

His teeth were bared, his solid legs trembling. But his eyes never left her face. As he pounded into her, she felt almost as if she floated free of her body, tethered only by his gaze.

The euphoria or pleasure grew into a towering wave, hovering, promising to break. Her legs ached and yet she couldn't stop. Couldn't slow. Reaching that crest was all that mattered. In a curling, slow-motion release of pressure almost too great to bear, she caught the edge, rockets of sensation shuddering into the very core of her being.

Throwing her head back under the onslaught, she allowed the pleasure to wash over her. Through her. Fully aware of Kashatok's muscles tightening, his huge hands holding her hips firmly, his release pumping into her with a force that took her breath away.

She slumped forward across his chest, completely spent, her ear pressed over his paired hearts. They raced in unison beneath her cheek. In that moment, she knew the bond truly was forever. She'd found the only purpose that really mattered.

Love.

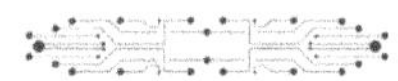

Not ready to end the adventures? Get the next book in the series, **Claimed by Noatak**, and keep reading now!

Dear Reader,

Thank you for joining Kashatok and Joy on this swash-buckling space adventure. In book three, **Claimed by Noatak**, we'll be back on the *Hardship* as the crews unite and put Joy's plan to find mates into action.

Gruff, no-nonsense Noatak's about to meet his match with a steely-eyed gunslinger...

Keep reading for an excerpt.

XOXO

Tamsin

P.S. Curious about what happened to Kashatok's first love, Aiyana? To find out, join my VIP Club and get an exclusive free prequel with Kashatok as a teenager. Sign up here> https://BookHip.com/SWNKJL

CLAIMED BY NOATAK

EXCERPT

Marlis leveled her Blackstar E-11 and squeezed the trigger. The target at the end of the range flashed three times. *Bulls-eye.*

"Fuck them and their standards," she muttered, pushing the target back another meter. She took aim and fired several more shots, each one flashing success. The E-11 zero-recoil pulse pistol had been a gift for her eleventh birthday, and after fourteen years and many other weapons, it was still her favorite. "I was even on time this morning."

"Good shot, Marlis!" Marlis's AI chimed from her wristband. The artificial intelligence was supposed to assist Marlis with anger management and lapses in memory, but its trite encouragements did nothing to assuage her today.

"Shut up, Twerp." Marlis racked the energy coil's cooling module and set the pistol aside. Picking up her customized Renegade MCS6 rifle, she reset the target for long-range and sighted in.

The lanes of the Syndicorp cruiser's firing range were all occupied today, but she had eyes only for her target, imagining each bulls-eye as the face of the service recruiter assigned to her file. *I'm Legacy, for fuck's sake.* Descended from a long line of trooper personnel with excellent records. And it wasn't as if she couldn't keep up during the drills. She could out-shoot, out-run, and out-wrestle every woman as well as most men in the squad. So what if she needed a little help to remember what day it was?

"Marlis!" a man's voice barked behind her.

Gut tightening, she whipped the rifle around.

Her father's narrow gaze flicked to the barrel, his mouth in a grim line as she lowered the weapon.

She refused to feel any regret about being battle-ready. Mom had died while she and Marlis had been on Pulati for a mother-daughter vacation. Ten-year-old Marlis had only survived the sudden terrorist outbreak by hiding beneath her mother's dead body for sixteen hours.

Marlis had no intention of letting her guard down. Ever.

Dad crossed his arms over his chest, covering the service ribbons on the lapel of his uniform. "You missed your date last night."

"That's tonight." Even as she said it, she realized she was probably wrong.

Twerp's feminine voice rose from her wrist strap. "I informed you of the engagement at seventeen hundred yesterday and again at seventeen twenty. You said you were in no mood to give someone a blow job and directed me not to remind you again."

Marlis's face heated to match the rising flush in her father's usually pallid cheeks. When would she ever remember to put in her earbud? Teeth clenched, she grated out, "Shut up, Twerp."

Dad squared his shoulders, looking Marlis straight in the eye. "He's a respectable young man, Marlis. From a good family. You couldn't ask for a better match."

"I don't want a better match. I want to join the troopers." She turned around and took aim at the target once more. "Get me a date with someone useful and I'll go."

"I can't rebuild the bridges you burn fast enough."

Refusing to be distracted, she let out a slow breath and squeezed the trigger in rapid succession. The target lit up on all but the final shot. She lowered the rifle. "I'd be a good soldier, Dad."

A gentle hand settled on her shoulder. "You blew up at your recruiter."

Marlis fuzzily remembered her rage at the small-eyed, beak-nosed recruiter who oversaw the drills the troopers used to weed out unworthy candidates. He was supposed to test the recruits' physical aptitudes. Instead, he'd thrown history questions at them. She seemed to recall a lot of swear words coming out of her mouth instead of answers. "What good is a history lesson going to do for me on the battle field?"

"He thinks you're a liability. They want to rescind your weapon carry permit." Dad's voice lowered with unaccustomed softness. "I'm sorry."

His words felt like a punch in the gut. Give up her pistol? *No way.* No longer able to focus on the target, Marlis shoved the E-11 into the holster built into the back hip of her pants and shouldered her rifle, turning to leave.

"Marlis."

She continued walking.

"Marlis. Your rifle case."

Face on fire, she halted; she might still have a permit to carry, but exiting the range actually welding a weapon, even on a military ship, was a big no-no. *Stupid memory.* Other AI models came equipped with a visual node to track items, but Marlis's therapist claimed that requiring her to remember some things on her own would help her improve.

Squaring her shoulders, she spun on her heel and retrieved the case, visually verifying there was nothing else she was leaving behind. Her father's watchful gaze made Marlis doubt herself. What else was she forgetting? *Dammit!*

Reacting to her elevated heart rate, Twerp vibrated against her wrist, encouraging her to remain calm, then came to the rescue with a reminder. "Marlis, you are scheduled for lunch with your sister in forty-three minutes. May I remind you that Attie is routinely early?"

"Thank you, Twerp." She offered her dad a weak smile. "I need to go clean up. I'll talk to you later."

Passing uniformed personnel as she moved through the carrier's corridors, Marlis silently repeated her mantra from years in therapy. *There is no danger.* Yet it was a hard mantra to believe when she'd just been told her right to carry a firearm was in jeopardy. She switched to *anger does more harm than good.* By the time she reached the family housing section and the modest quarters she shared with her dad and sister, Twerp had stopped buzzing.

She stowed her rifle and washed her face, then headed toward the mess hall on the lower deck where Attie probably already waited. Her big sister had been accepted into the troopers over a year ago, quickly rising to Private First Class. The job left Attie little time to visit with family, although she made a point of having lunch weekly with Marlis. No matter how routine it might be, Marlis's heart lightened at the thought of seeing her.

Uniform crisp and ash-blonde hair trimmed to short ringlets, Attie was already seated at their usual table. The huge room echoed with the predominantly human lunch crowd filling long tables, the homogeny interspersed by a few clusters of aliens. Attie's head was down, eyes scanning the screen of a polycom as Marlis approached. A new gold chevron adorned the epaulet on her shoulder.

"You made corporal?" Marlis asked, unable to drag her gaze from the emblem.

Attie set the polycom aside and rose, brushing her fingertips over the rank badge before rounding the table to give Marlis a hug. "I officially got the promotion today."

"Hugging's against regulation. They're gonna come take that chevron back." Marlis squeezed her sister, trying to summon a sense of humor instead of jealousy. Her sister was so together.

Attie rolled her eyes and once more took her seat. She glanced toward the long chow line. "You want to go first while I finish these reports?"

Nodding, Marlis got in line among the uniformed personnel. Prior to this moment, she'd always strutted into the mess hall knowing she was among her people; it was only a matter of time before she had her own uniform. Now it felt like everyone's eyes were on her; challenging her worth.

Putting two plates onto her tray, she selected the chicken curry and skipped the dessert section, opting for two coffees with cream instead. Although Attie never asked, Marlis always came back with food for both of them. It seemed like a waste of precious sister-time to send Attie to stand in line all over again.

Returning to the table, Marlis set both plates down. "It was this or something that looked like cat vomit."

"Thanks." Attie picked up her fork and poked at a sliced tomato, edging it away from her chicken. "How're things with Dad?"

Something about the set of Attie's shoulders had Marlis on edge. "He's still trying to set me up with Colonel Yan's son. Why do you ask?"

Attie shrugged. "Is he cute?"

Now Marlis's warning bells began to chime. "Some people think so. Why?"

Taking a big bite, Attie chewed slowly before answering. "You turn twenty-six soon. You know what that means."

Of course she knew. At twenty-six, she'd lose her status as her father's dependent and all the perks that came with it. Unless she joined the troopers herself, she'd be sent to ground, forced to join the civilians on one muddy planet or another. Trapped, just like on Pulati. *Never, never, never.* "Of course I do. What does that have to do with Colonel Yan's son?"

"A lot of people enjoy marriage. It'd give you a partner."

"Marrying some douche bag I could beat at arm wrestling won't solve my problems."

Attie tapped her fork against her plate nervously. "Marlis, you need someone you can rely on."

"What do you mean? I have you. And I have Dad when he's not being a dick."

Setting her fork down, Attie took a deep breath, gaze locked with Marlis's. "I've been assigned to the flagship Icarus."

It felt as if someone had just opened the ship's blast doors, sucking away all the oxygen. Marlis's vision narrowed, the room fading around her. *Attie can't leave.* Her sister was her rock. The one person she could always turn to. Twerp buzzed almost painfully against her skin, telling her to calm down.

Attie leaned forward, speaking slowly. "It's part of my promotion. A great opportunity for advancement. I'll be serving on Admiral Olly's primary staff."

Marlis gulped. "I don't see you enough as it is."

"It'll be okay." Attie reached across the table and covered Marlis's hand with hers. "We can still talk on the vid. And Dad says—" She cut off, biting a corner of her lip as if she'd said too much.

"You told Dad already?" Marlis choked out. She'd always been Attie's confidante, the first to hear anything. "Before me?"

"He's worried about you, Marlis. You're his baby. He even called James."

Their older brother, James, had left when Marlis was ten, before she'd gone to Pulati with Mom. He was currently a Staff Sergeant on Aleigh. "What does James have to do with me?"

"He's trying to get you a dependency waiver. It's easier on planetary bases."

"You mean live with James?" Marlis shot to her feet, her blood on fire. "You're kidding me!" People at surrounding tables turned to stare. Twerp vibrated doggedly against her wrist. Still, Marlis couldn't keep her voice down. "And you agree with him?"

"No." Attie kept level contact with Marlis's eyes, exuding confidence. "Sit down, please."

"There is no danger, Marlis," Twerp added.

"Shut the fuck up, Twerp." There *was* danger. It was all around her, from places she never expected. "Dad says they're going to take away my weapon carry permit."

"What? They can't!" Attie's calm demeanor broke, and she rose to her feet.

Oddly enough, that made Marlis feel better. "I had an argument with my recruiter." Heat filled her face, and she lowered herself slowly back to her seat, scrubbing a hand over her forehead. "Do you think they'll let me petition for another try?"

Attie sighed, looking down at her little sister a moment before shaking her head no. "I won't lie to you. I've heard talk that you're unstable."

For the first time she could remember, Marlis felt tears prick her eyes. Actual, honest-to-god tears. She hated it. "What am I going to do?"

Picking up the polycom beside her plate, Attie began tapping in commands. "Since you can't live on board the carrier after your birthday and you don't want to live with James," she set the device on the tabletop and shoved it toward Marlis, "I think you should look for a job."

Marlis stared at the polycom, her pulse thundering in her ears. *A job?* As in something other than working for the troopers? Her brain refused to transform the blocks of text on the screen into meaningful information. "What is this?"

"Ads for jobs on Whylon Station. There are other options for you than military service. Legit shipping businesses looking for hired guns. Bodyguards. That kind of thing."

"Not through the troopers?" Marlis frowned. "Don't companies contract through the corp' for those services?"

Her sister laughed and retrieved the polycom. "There's a world outside of Syndicorp—whole regions of the galaxy, in fact. Not everyone can afford troopers. You're fantastic with weapons, Sis. And you want to protect people. Let's find a way for you to do it." Attie stood. "I have to go or I'll be late for duty. I forwarded you the info." She took a few steps away, then looked over her shoulder and winked. "Oh, and don't tell Dad I suggested this, okay? I'd like to keep my reputation as the good daughter."

Watching her sister's retreating back, Marlis repeated her mantra. *There is no danger.* Yet she couldn't manage to take a full breath, let alone pull out her own polycom. *Work other than with the service?*

"Would you like me to assist?" Twerp asked calmly.

Grateful for any help she could get, Marlis nodded. "Yeah. Tell me about these shipping companies."

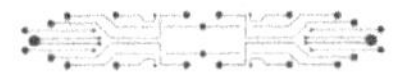

Get Claimed by Noatak and keep reading now!

Glossary

•*Anaq* - Shit

•*Akleng* - a term of sympathy or regret, poor baby

•**Attahat wheel** - A form of gambling using a random wheel much like roulette

•**Burn** - The means by which ships travel long distances quickly using ionic frequencies to bend space

•**Carayak** - A male denaidan with a genetic disorder that causes his ionic mating frequency to be deadly even to his own kind. Literally translated as "monster"

•**Cartel** - Organized crime ring

•**Cirripi weed** - Used as a mild intoxicant when smoked

•**Cochlear implant** - A cybernetic device that transmits

communications via vibrations directly against the bones of the ear

•**Darkweb** - A place used by the cartel and other black market entities to exchange information

•**Denaida-daru** - The denaidan home world, destroyed by Syndicorp. Also called planet K-4H10

•*Ellam Cua* - The denaidan deity

•**Enayshuan** - A human-like species with prominent eye ridges, known for their metallic body powder. Often associated with the sex trade

•**Finofan** - Aliens with iguana-like frills around their ears and slitted eyes. They like hot and humid atmosphere

•**Garan'uk** - A methane breathing alien species

•*Iluq* - Brother

•**Ionic power or shield** - A denaidan ability to affect matter and gravity

•**Kemeg** - A type of herd animal raised for its meat

•**Kwirn** - A form of gambling using 3-D tables and pieces

•**Nanites** - Micro-computers used for a variety of purposes

•**Naujiar** - A type of plant. Also a netorpok's preferred food

•**Nav-grav seats** - Used to keep humanoids comfortable during ship burn

•**Netorpok** - An exotic pet banned on most worlds

•**Ongaru Flip** - A popular card game

•**Parsec** - A measurement of distance (3.2 light years)

•**Pirelux silk** - A fine fabric

•**Polycom** - The most common form of personal communication and information storage, much like today's smartphone

•**Posungi** - An egg-laying alien with an orange tentacled face

•*Qumli* - Asshole

•**Rakwiji** - Scaled aliens with a poisonous claw, who hunt in pairs and require torture as part of their mating ritual. Often hired by the cartel as bounty hunters

•**Sizantha pods** - Used to make tea

•**Syndicorp** - A mega-corporation that runs a huge section of the galaxy

•**The Termination** - Syndicorp's destruction of Denaida-daru

•***Ucuk*** - Dick

•***Uminaq*** - Dammit

•**Unclassified space** - Areas of the galaxy not ruled by Syndicorp

•**Xeimir worm** - A glossy-skinned alien that breathes through its skin and is ultra-sensitive to light

•**Yanipa-nimayu** - A six-legged alien often found performing manual labor

About the Author

Once upon a time I thought I wanted to be a biomedical engineer, but experimenting on lab rats doesn't always lead to happy endings. Instead, I turned my nerdy fascination with science into stories filled with alien pirates, monsters, and character-driven romance with guaranteed happily-ever-afters.

My books feature feisty heroines, tortured heroes, and just enough science fiction or magic to get them into all kinds of steamy trouble. My monsters always find their mates—and I promise my stories will never leave you hanging (although you may still crave more).

When I'm not writing, you'll probably find me in the garden or the kitchen, exploring Alaska with my husband, or preparing for the zombie apocalypse. I also enjoy crocheting while binge-watching Netflix, playing video games, and spending family time during our weekly D&D sessions.

Want more stories from my worlds?

Join my VIP Club to receive free books, bonus scenes, sneak peeks, and exclusive updates.

https://www.tamsinley.com/join-club

bookbub.com/authors/tamsin-ley

goodreads.com/TamsinLey

facebook.com/TamsinLey

amazon.com/author/tamsin